Dixie Luck

Terminal is a bittersweet tale of two stubborn, independent souls searching for security and a respite from the solitude they seem unable to surrender. It is also an evocative snapshot of a particular kind of life in New Orleans—one lived far from the decadence and dazzle, the bon temps of Mardi Gras, or touring the Quarter.
—Julia Glass, author of *A House Among the Trees,*
I See You Everywhere and
National Book Award winner
Three Junes

MERCER UNIVERSITY PRESS

Endowed by

TOM WATSON BROWN
and
THE WATSON-BROWN FOUNDATION, INC.

Dixie Luck

Stories and the novella Terminal

Andy Plattner

For Nancy,
Best of luck,
Andy Plattner

MERCER UNIVERSITY PRESS | *Macon, Georgia*

2018

MUP/ P560

© 2018 by Mercer University Press
Published by Mercer University Press
1501 Mercer University Drive
Macon, Georgia 31207

9 8 7 6 5 4 3 2 1

Books published by Mercer University Press are printed on
acid-free paper that meets the requirements of the American
National Standard for Information Sciences—Permanence of
Paper for Printed Library Materials.

ISBN   978-0-88146-651-5
Cataloging-in-Publication Data is available from the Library
of Congress

Printed in Canada

For Diana.

And our pals, Melanie and Steve.

Winner of the 2017 Ferrol Sams Award for Fiction

Contents

Acknowledgments

Many thanks to many good souls: Cara Blue Adams, Frederick Barthelme, George Core, Dixie/Eggs/Joe, John Henry Fleming, Julia Glass, Tony Grooms, John Holman, Rosemary James / Faulkner Society, Marc Jolley / Mercer University Press, Michael Koch, Gary McMillen, Emily Nemens, and Anna Schachner.

On any number of occasions, the real racehorse Skyring brought me what felt like all the luck in the world.

I also express my thanks to the original publishers of some of the stories in this collection:

EPOCH : "Blazer," "Resort Life"

FOLIO : "Prodigy"

New World Writing : "Application," "Hot Springs," "Library"

The Southern Review : "Confetti," "Valdosta"

William Faulkner / William Wisdom Writing Competition Gold Medal for Novella : *Terminal*

Dixie Luck

Hot Springs

As I was looking over my program, I heard a woman's voice say my name. I took a second before I said, "Catherine." Then I looked up. "This is my friend Darren," she said. The man standing next to her offered a nod. Beyond the panes of the glassed-in grandstand, winter sunlight brightened the dingy white rails of the racing oval. This was the second day of the meet. The day before, I'd seen Catherine—whose nickname was Chick when I'd dated her—sitting with this guy. I'd had Denice Bejarano with me and I kept away from them. Today I was by myself and wanted to sit closer. A year and a half ago, when Chick and I were sharing a motel room in Lafayette, Louisiana, she stole three grand from me. She took the money and split, left me a note that said she'd gone to Memphis to get an abortion. But it was all smoke. I didn't want to raise a family. I would have driven her to Memphis myself.

I said, "You doing any good?"

Darren looked mid-forties, older than her by a decade. Slender man with gray at his temples. Chick, a tall woman, wore a snug dress with a green-and-blue pattern. Maybe she wasn't working on the backstretch anymore. She took his arm and they smiled at one another. I noticed their hands were clean of rings and she wore more makeup than I remembered. "I'm the horseplayer," she said. "How about you?"

"Start of a meet. I'm just trying to see what the trends are."

"Of course," she said.

I held over my program. "Here, mark it for me." I was smiling; I didn't know if Darren understood. Chick hesitated, then she took the program and began to turn the pages. The third race was coming up.

She turned to check the electronic odds board, out in the infield. The grass there was khaki and dry and the dogwood trees along the backstretch were not yet in bloom. "I do have a couple of horses I like," she said. "Pen, sweetheart." I knew she wasn't talking to me, so I didn't move. For some reason, Darren tapped at his waist. She reached for his shirt pocket.

Chick wrote on a page of the program. "I work at the barns back there," I said to Darren. "Assistant foreman. We just shipped in from New Mexico." I understood that Chick was listening. I wasn't assistant anything. I was a groom for a trainer named Forster who'd just run out on a bunch of bills in Albuquerque. I'd shipped to Hot Springs with Denice, a woman I knew just well enough. She had been married to the same guy for twenty years, but they'd broken up. Back in the Q, she worked at a community college, though she had recently lost her job there. At night, she went to some of the same bars I did. We got along well, especially at night, and one of the things she liked about me was that I was not a "baggage guy" and that I seemed like a bit of a badass. On a lark, she decided to try Hot Springs. But she was hedging her bets. She kept up the rent on her apartment back in Albuquerque; probably had a Greyhound schedule in her back pocket.

"Maybe you ought to be giving tips to us," Darren said, after moments when no one said a word. He didn't look completely stupid. Maybe he figured I wanted something. I probably looked like a bottom feeder to him.

"The horses we have…," I said. Then I stopped and I shook my head once, which I thought Chick could see from the corner of her eye. "Probably going to be a long winter." It didn't hurt to acknowledge it, not right then.

Chick closed the program, held it over to me. She recapped the pen and stuck it in Darren's shirt pocket. He looked happy about something. I opened the program, nodded my head, flipped over one page, then another. "I'll keep an eye on these," I said.

"No promises," she said. "Right, Darren?"

"Not at this place," he said. He didn't appear to be a barn worker and I guessed he might be a horse owner. Owners could afford to lose, or so they believed, and sometimes they came off as superior. I understood this was as close as Chick and Darren wanted me to be. Maybe they were in love.

"No," I said. "Not here." In the program, where the horses for the sixth race were listed, Chick had written a phone number. I closed the program, waved it, and said, "Advice is always welcome."

"We wanted to say hi," she said. "Didn't want you to think I didn't know you."

"Good luck," he said.

"Good luck," I said.

Chick twiddled her fingers in my direction, took his arm, and they turned and moved along. They must've gone to a beer stand or the oyster bar near the track gift shop because their seats stayed empty. I focused on the races, though I hadn't brought enough cash to play in a meaningful way. I hadn't shipped over here with much. In the past, I had worked for bigger stables, though I was just a number at all of them. I had ideas about certain horses, but I couldn't get my superiors to listen. Those outfits always paid on time. The guy I worked for now, he gave us our wages in cash— when he had it. He was always open to suggestions, had said as much to me. I guessed there was a variety of ways to interpret that, but I knew if I could spot an angle, we all would benefit.

I didn't feel like hanging around for the feature. My concentration wasn't what it needed to be, and besides there were plenty of race days ahead. I walked down to the ground-floor level and out

3

through the turnstiles toward my trusty Chevy Celebrity. I switched on the radio, caught a Pearl Jam cover of "I'm Waiting for the Man," and drove up the road a mile to my motel, the Cottonland Arms. I pulled into the slip right outside the room. When I unlocked the door and pushed it open, I saw Denice standing at the mirror over the sink at the far end of the room. She was just out of the shower, wore a towel around her head and another around her torso. She must've heard me pull up because she didn't turn, simply watched me in the mirror. The Celeb's engine did have a ping—it made me think of the guitar intro for "Where the Streets Have No Name."

I walked over and sat on the edge of the bed. In the trashbasket by the TV stand was an empty can of Raid, which I hoped had done its job. Yesterday, we'd seen a spider in the room. It crawled out from under the bed right after I returned from my morning shift. It was smaller than the palm of my hand—still a pretty nasty-looking thing. I dropped a phone book on it. Denice wanted to complain to the manager, but I told her this would be a waste of time so we drove around until we found a can of Raid strong enough to kill scorpions. I dropped her off at a bar close to our motel, then went to spray our room. A room like this always takes some breaking in. I blasted everything, the base of the walls, the corners, the threshold of the door.

Just across from the foot of the bed was a bureau with a rectangular mirror hanging above it. Motel rooms generally have lights that are too bright and there are too many mirrors overall, but there's nothing you can do about it. I watched my reflection as I said, "Saw an old friend who owes me a few thousand. I think they're good for it."

"Really."

I shrugged. "Yeah," I said. "I caught 'em at a good time, it looks like."

"Them?"

"Her. The one I was kind of watching yesterday."

Denice didn't say anything, just pulled the towel off her head. Her curly, brown-gray hair looked metallic when it was wet.

I said, "I think that's the key, just catching people at the right time." I took out my cell phone, consulted the number Chick had written in my racing program. I texted her: *can we talk*. Denice sat next to me and I held up the program, pointed to the number. It occurred to me that Chick probably gave me the number of a local diaper service. I didn't say this—a bad joke, even if it would be lost on Denice. "Maybe it's a bail bondsman," I said.

"How does a woman come to owe you a few thousand, slick?"

I said, "The short answer is that we weren't right for each other."

"You guys are charging a fee for that now?"

"She waited until I had a decent hit at the track, then picked me clean. Closest thing she'd ever get to a fortune, that's for sure. What would you do, let her off the hook? If it'll impress you, I will."

"You need the money?"

"I could use it."

In a moment, she said, "Make her pay." Her voice was pretty quiet, though.

"You get the clock radio to work?" In the mirror the radio was behind me, its digits still dark.

"Somebody must've spilled something on it. I called the front desk, but the guy said he didn't have any extras."

"We pay by the month," I said. "Outside of new sheets and towels, this is an island. Anyway, got a great place picked out for dinner." I leaned into her, kissed at the freckled, faintly wrinkled skin under her collarbone. I ran the back of my hand along her hip and the towel felt coarse.

5

Denice looked at my hand and I took it away. She said, "Please, fetch me a clock radio. I'm not like you. I need an alarm. Go. Try please."

I stood, "Okay, okay. I'll be in the lobby."

I closed the door behind me and went up the sidewalk. At the track, it was nearly time for the feature. The better, more reliable horses ran in the feature, and if you weren't trying to make up for big losses earlier on the card, it was usually a manageable race. The nightcap, the race after that, was when the riders occasionally played their games. They held horses, let the crazy longshots win. Most of the time, the horses in the last race were running for the cheapest purse of the day, and they were wildly unreliable to start with.

That tri I hit in Lafayette—the money Chick swiped—was from a Saturday nightcap. Basically, I just handicapped the race upside down, searched for any reason in the world to play the outsiders. Sometimes you get lucky when you look at things that way. Chick had stayed away from the races that day, or more specifically away from me, and when I came back to our room, she was sitting up, watching TV. I tossed the pile of money onto the bed, wanted her to feel better about everything. Later, after she was gone, I understood I'd practically dared her to steal it.

The motel lobby stood adjacent to the registration area, offering a knock-off brand flat screen and a counter with a coffee pot they kept full. I went right to the rack that had all the pamphlets about local attractions and restaurants. Some advertised mineral baths and massages, and then I found one from McClard's Barbecue; going by the menu, I could afford the place. The pamphlet offered a positive testimonial from F. Murray Abraham. Denice and I had seen him in *The Grand Budapest Hotel* and she'd loved it. I memorized the address, went over to make myself a cup of coffee, sat on the couch, and looked at the soccer game playing on the TV, which was turned down low. No one was behind the registration counter, but in a minute I heard muffled laughter coming from a closed door. The guy who ran the Cottonland probably lived here, had a wife and so on. Beyond that door, there might have been all kinds of hallways and hidden rooms. Maybe it was like a whole house.

I fantasized about owning a motel myself someday. But there would be so many rooms to keep track of. One thing I knew for sure was that if you were living in a motel room with someone else, you needed to give them space. I'd seen Denice in and out of her clothes plenty already, but that had little to do with privacy. Sometimes a room didn't feel big enough to me, and that could produce a taste of panic. At least this type of panic faded—that was something I could always count on. I knew that a motel room had everything, and when it was time to go, there wasn't a lot to hold you there.

I heard a tapping at the window that looked out to the street. Denice stood there in a steel-gray blouse and jeans, her hair dry now, with big curls that fell to her shoulders. "Where's my radio?" she said, her breath fogging a place on the glass.

I gave a thumbs-up.

At the barbecue place, we were seated at a table for two right beneath a color 8x10 of Bill and Hillary, each of them tilting a full platter towards the camera. They were much younger. Denice and I were looking at the photo when the waitress arrived, her pencil out. Denice gestured toward the Clintons and said, "Do a lot of people just point to the picture and say, 'I'll have what they are having'?"

The waitress, who had a kind face, said, "Actually, yes."

"And beer," I said, indicating Denice and myself.

"I can do that for you," the waitress said.

The platters of food were just like the ones in the photo: barbecue, beans, mac and cheese, and cole slaw—everything touching everything. We ate without saying much. Then my cell went off, showing the number I'd texted. I answered, and Chick's voice said, "Look, you can't follow me around like that." I didn't feel like defending myself, not with Denice there. "Where are you?"

"McClard's," I said. "This place is full of winners." My eyes went to Denice. I pointed to the phone, then made an imaginary dollar sign in the air. "So, look," I said.

"Play nice," Chick said.

I thought for a second, then said, "Exactly." I balled up my napkin and tossed it onto my empty plate. Denice was not as far along with her platter, had just cleaned out her cole slaw.

"I want to make things straight," Chick said. "I've got five hundred in my purse. I'll bring it to you tomorrow. Not at the track, though."

"It's more than that, Chick," I said. "You know it." Denice held her fork over her barbecue and mouthed the word *Chick?*

The restaurant was noisy, and what I heard Chick saying was, "You wanted me to have all of it…gift wrapped."

"I'm with a shaky outfit, man. I already told you." Silence. "Hello?" I said.

"I'll bring what I can," Chick finally said. "After that, when you see me coming, you gotta duck, you have to run for cover. I like this guy I'm with."

"Who, Darren?"

"I'm already halfway tempted to tell him what's going on. You can just deal with him."

Darren looked like his scrapping-over-a-woman days were behind him, but I didn't say this. "I'm staying at the Cottonland," I said. "Room sixteen. How about noon tomorrow?" I glanced at Denice.

"Settled. Bye."

I kept the phone by my ear after Chick hung up. I thought of something to say into it, something that might make it appear like I was in control. "Okay, see ya," I said. I set the phone by my platter. "Still in negotiation."

"Chick?" Denice said. "Her name is Chick?"

"Nickname."

"What's yours? Fella?"

"I was called Ace in high school."

"I bet you were."

"What about you?" I was anxious to change the subject. "Nickname-wise, I mean."

Denice had her elbows on the table. The question seemed to catch her off guard, and I could almost see her thoughts moving around. She'd worked as a professor, but with me she usually had more questions than anything. The whole Chick episode felt a little unwelcome just then. "On-Her-Knees-Denice," she said. "I gave my first hummer when I was like fourteen years old. Guilty." Her expression was thoughtful. "I went away to college, so I got to start all over again. Nickname-wise."

"You turned out good, though," I said.

"Oh?"

"You wound up working at a college."

She watched me for a second. In a moment, her expression seemed sympathetic. "You still like Girl or whatever her name is, don't you? Don't be a dick. Just tell the truth." I didn't say anything and she seemed satisfied. "I'm still in love with my ex-husband," she said, almost matter-of-factly. "Kind of." Her eyes went to the condiments at the middle of our table. Bottles of Tabasco, ketchup, Worchestershire, mini-jalapenos. "But he knows that."

I nodded.

"You're going to let her off easy," she said.

"I'm not going to just follow her around for the whole meeting," I said. "Look, tomorrow's the last of it."

She moved her fork. "You shouldn't make those kinds of promises."

Denice didn't eat half of what was on her plate, and I wondered if she might be in the mood for something else. When we got back to the motel, she went to the bathroom and I turned off the lights, had the TV going with the sound down. She had a black teddy she liked to wear but hadn't unpacked it yet. When she came out of the bathroom, the light from the TV gave her nude body a mauve color. I felt woozy and she seemed like a hologram. She faced the mirror with her hands on her hips, and I guessed she wanted to see what was behind her. "I don't feel like doing it in the bed, tonight, okay?" she said.

"Okay."

"Turn off that goddamn TV. You don't know me and you don't know my name. I want you to lie on the floor and I don't want you to say a thing."

"All right."

"Try not to speak."

"I heard you."

"Come over here."

I lay on the floor, and it was easy to concentrate on her. My hands were flat on the carpet, and once I was inside her she liked to go slow so I could feel everything about her. I felt her like that and the backs of my hands tingled. I thought about that spider from the day before and flexed my hands. She started to ride; she whispered things, said, "It's not time, it's not time...here we go..."

When we climbed into bed later, she asked if anything was up with me, and for a second I felt irritated, like saying, *Am I just a dick to you?* I didn't say anything, didn't want to have a discussion like that. Overall, I guessed I was starting to feel a little unlucky.

Around 4 A.M., I awakened without an alarm and turned on the light on the nightstand. Denice didn't stir. I went to the little bureau beyond the foot of the bed, took out my work clothes, and changed in the bathroom. I turned off the nightstand light before I left. I closed the door as quietly as possible, turned the knob in my hand to make sure the lock was firm. I drove for the track under the inky night sky, passed the silhouettes of franchise business signs. Hot Springs was a racetrack town, but horse racing was a dying sport and I always had to be careful about my expectations. The track was at the center of things, and beyond it, in the direction we'd come from, were the resort hotels, the old bath houses. The big hotels were likely to be the emptiest ones; we'd agreed on that as we were driving in.

By the time I finished my morning shift at the barn, the sky looked pale blue but the air was still pretty cold. I pulled into the same space outside our room, turned off the Celeb, walked to the door, took off my boots, held them by the ankles and tapped at my pockets for my key card. The bed was made and there was a piece of paper sitting in the middle of it. It was a slip from a motel pad with the Cottonland's logo printed at the top, a sun either rising or setting beyond a line of mountains, which I guessed were the Caddos or the Blue Ouachitas. I thought it might be a kiss-off from Denice, and it took a second for my eyes to focus.

Took a walk. Probably be back after a while.

I tried to figure out how mad she was, see if I could tell something from the handwriting. Just simple, printed letters, like I wouldn't be able to understand otherwise. I took a bath, sat upright for a time, even though the water wasn't hot enough and the tub was too small for me to keep my legs straight. I didn't feel particularly clean after all this.

I put on nice clothes, a brown western-cut shirt and blue jeans, and was sitting in the chair at the little table for two near the door when I heard a knock. It was before noon, I knew that. I opened the door to Chick, in a dark-blue wool jacket and jeans, her hands in the pockets of her jacket. Beyond my car was a blue Saab, a driver behind the wheel: Darren, facing straight ahead.

"Here," Chick said and handed over a folded stack of bills that could not be three grand. "Take it." She kept her eyes on my face. "I told him everything. He kind of laughed about it." My eyes went out to Darren again. "You need to stay away from us." She stood on her toes, looked past my shoulder. The bed was made; no one else was here. She cut her eyes to me. "I got out at the right time. You can't deny that."

I wasn't going to. "What kind of place do you have?" I said. She didn't say anything. "What's he do?" I said.

"A syndicate manager. A bunch of doctors in Maryland have a string of horses down here." She shrugged. "He helps find the best races for them. I met him last fall. We're down here for the winter." I thought about taking her by the arm, pulling her into the room and closing the door. I wanted to talk to her. Maybe if that was just another groom waiting in the car for her, I would've done it. I felt the money in my hand.

"We okay?" she said.

"That money," I said. "I was telling you something."

"You were trying to do me a favor then," she said. "It's a shame you don't see it that way now." She nodded to the money she'd given me. "You never really expect anything. Despite the way you present yourself. So you're grateful for the smallest thing." She had a look in her eye then, like she was superior and sorrowful all at once. "See ya," she said. Hands back in pockets, she turned and walked past my Celeb to the Saab. She got in on the passenger side and they drove off. I closed the door, stepped back and counted the bills. Five hundred bucks. I counted it again, wanted to feel indignant. A few days ago, I couldn't have predicted that I would even see Chick here, let alone get anything out of her. *Grateful.* It sounded like an accusation. The word stuck in the back of my throat. I guessed she wanted me to hate her just a little. I had this money in my hand and I wanted to feel all right about it. I wasn't unhappy with my life; I could do something else if I wanted. I didn't mind juggling racetracks and women because solutions to everything always felt so close at hand. At some point, I sat on the edge of the bed and I might have stayed there for a little while. One obvious truth was that I'd felt more for Chick than I'd ever cared to admit. I thought about throwing the money on the bed when we had been sharing a room together. That should've been a good moment.

I didn't want to be sitting on the bed feeling defeated so I clicked on the TV, flipped channels for a minute, then turned it off again. I went to the bathroom counter, brushed my teeth, combed my hair with my hand, then pulled on my boots and stepped outside. I started the Celeb and dialed Denice to see where she might be. When she answered, I heard the sound of the wind blowing. Cars were going by, too—I could hear as much. There weren't any sidewalks along our stretch of highway so I said, "Let me pick you up right now."

"Hang a right leaving the motel lot," her voice said. "You can't miss me." Outside, the sky had turned sand-colored and I drove for a minute past the telephone poles and business signs, found myself wondering if this winter could be a good one. She was walking on the shoulder, away from our motel. I had to pull beyond her and wait for her to catch up. She wore her brown-and-black checked jacket and her hair was blowing all around. She got in on the passenger side, and I dropped my hands from the wheel. "I got five hundred," I said.

Her expression didn't reveal much. "Let me see it," she said, taking the bills. "Hundreds. You know what that means, don't you?" Cars swooshed past us and the Celeb rocked. "She had more."

"Nothing is really on the books, you know?" I said. "That's the problem." I thought she would say something to this and was glad she didn't. I glanced at the side mirror, decided to pull out.

"Oh, I really don't feel like going to the track today," Denice said.

We were headed in that direction, and I said, "I don't really feel like it, either."

"Bullshit," she said. "Here." She held the money out to me. My first instinct was to say *Take something for yourself*, but Denice wasn't a racetracker. I put the thin stack in my pocket. I wondered if I should ask where she was walking to or what she had been thinking about. Traffic slowed as we neared the track, and she kept her eyes in the direction of the brick grandstand.

When we were past that, I said, "We can go right on Route 12, drive to Little Rock. See the Clinton Museum."

She shrugged. "I don't vote."

We were already heading in the direction of the older downtown area, toward the places that once offered mineral baths and now had historical signs in front of them. "I think a couple of the hotels up there still have open spas," I said. "Pretty sure the Hot Springs Resort does." Denice seemed curious about the bath houses we passed. It had warmed up a little, was early afternoon now. On our way in a few days earlier, we'd seen these old spas, but we'd been searching for our motel then. We stopped at a red light and I said, "Let me treat you."

"What would I have to do?" she said.

I shrugged. "Nothing. The Hot Springs Resort is right up here." It was a huge hotel with a granite facade, a dozen floors, a bronze-like dome. It had to be the biggest hotel in Arkansas. She didn't say anything as I turned toward it. When we pulled into the hotel's half-circle driveway, I wheeled us to the entrance and a valet appeared, a young black guy in a loose-looking maroon jacket. He held the door for Denice but she didn't get out of the car. "The baths are open, right?" I said.

"Yep," he said. "Second floor."

"Go on," I said to her. "I'll park the car and then go up there and wait for you."

"You're not going to get a massage?"

"Maybe I will," I said. "They'll take care of you." The kid who'd opened the door for her seemed cautious. "Here," I said, and wiggled the money back out of my pocket. I gave her a hundred, then nodded to the kid, said, "I need to get some change."

As she headed for the glass doors of the hotel entrance, the kid stayed one step in front of her. He held the door and I decided to get going. I could have let him park the car, but then when we came out of the baths he'd have to bring it back for me. I'd have to tip him twice and I didn't want to seem like some big shot.

Farther down the street was metered parking, and I found a couple of quarters at the bottom of a cup holder. When I walked into the lobby of the Hot Springs Resort, the kid was there, standing at the registration desk, talking to the guy working behind the counter. The lobby had marble floors; looking out to Central Avenue was a cocktail lounge with sofas and a bar counter with a half-dozen stools in front of it. Behind the counter, a frosted mirror went all the way to the ceiling. The elevators were across the lobby. I took one up, stepped out on the second floor onto a red-carpeted hallway, and followed a sign, made a right, went all the way to the end of another hallway. I opened a door at the end of it and

15

stepped into a waiting-room area where the chairs had leatherette seats and backs, chrome arms and legs. Right away, I thought of the barbershop my old man had taken me to, back when I still had someone telling me what to do. A large woman with short red hair sat behind a counter and I said, "I'm just gonna wait for my friend. She came in here a few minutes ago, I think." The walls were white. Near the woman, white towels were stacked on room-service carts. "What are they going to do to her back there?" I said. The woman blinked, then she pointed to a brochure on the counter.

I took a chair in the waiting area, read about the 100-degree baths, how hot packs were applied to "particularly stressful areas" and so on. Following a shower came an optional full-body Swedish massage. I hoped Denice got that. We hadn't been in the area long, and I guessed she didn't as yet have a positive view of Hot Springs. If she could hang around until spring, she'd see how pretty the backstretch was when the dogwoods were in bloom. At the end of the meet was Arkansas Derby week, and I imagined the stands would really be rocking.

I could've been back there getting a massage, too—that wasn't lost on me—but the cost of it would've meant that much less in my pocket when I went to the races. Playing the horses influenced the way I looked at money and how it could work for me. It wasn't that I didn't deserve something good like a hot springs bath and a massage, it's just I didn't see how it could change anything. That was the way I tended to look at life's luxuries. It might seem like a sad outlook from a distance, and one day, when my luck turned for good, I probably would take a different view. But there was no sense in fooling myself until that happened.

My eyes closed at one point because I was thinking of things so intently and felt a bit tired, too. I sensed something close to my face. Through a half-open eye I saw Denice, with a sympathetic expression. She had her hair tied back and the same clothes she'd worn when she'd been walking along the highway. Over her right forearm was her brown-and-black checked jacket, along with a folded white cotton robe. "Ready?" she said.

"Time?" I said. I stood up too fast and she helped to balance me.

"Yep." She waved in the direction of the lady behind the counter. "Bye, Marcy," she said.

"Good-bye," the lady said.

Denice and I walked down the hallway. "You stealing that robe?"

"Complimentary," she said.

I touched the call button for the elevator and felt like asking her about the bath and the massage but didn't. She could talk about it when she wanted. We rode the elevator down, and once we were out in the lobby, she tucked the folded robe between her knees and started to pull on her coat. "I can hold that," I said, but then she had her jacket on and the bunched-up white robe was secured under her arm like a football.

"We're over here," I said, and we began to walk up the sidewalk. Once we were in the Celeb, she sat in the passenger seat, let out an exhale, leaned over and kissed my cheek. I thought she was going to say thanks but then I was glad she didn't. It was the middle of the afternoon and I detected the faintest of blue in the sky.

She seemed to be studying my profile. Then, she bowed her head, picked at the belt of the robe. "I heard a couple of the attendants talking about horses," she said. "Like the two horse in the eighth race today or something. Just a couple of old gals. They said a trainer had been in there earlier..." Her voice trailed off, then she said, "Just first drop me off at the motel." The robe was in her lap and her arms were folded over it.

"Sure," I said. I started the car, made a U-turn right there on Central, and we drove past the resort. The sky was silvery now and the sun was at our backs as we rode down Central Avenue. I thought of myself in a huge porcelain bathtub, my arms hanging off the sides. I thought of attendants standing there, waiting with folded towels. My eyes went to the robe, and after a second she dropped her arm closer to her side.

"Go on, you can touch it," she said.

"Just for luck," I said. I wanted to show her I wasn't afraid of anything. I moved my hand over the collar. It was soft, pleasant.

"Tough guy," she said.

"Right," I said, though my voice was pretty quiet. I tried to think of something positive then. I would be at the track soon. Even if I didn't feel like I was going to win anything, sometimes it was better to just go on and go.

Application

In early spring, after a night of drinking at the Primrose Tavern, Chet swerved his Lexus onto his own front lawn and crashed into the trunk of the about-to-bloom sugar maple. He pulled himself out of the car, and decided to take a piss while standing directly in the still-beaming headlights. Across the street, lights went on in one house, then another. Donna, the woman Chet lived with, jogged across the yard and tried to get him inside. Someone called the police and, at age fifty-nine, he was arrested for the first time in his life. Drunk and disorderly. Donna, twenty jears his junior, bailed him out in the morning. They drove the Lexus through the quiet streets in their Marietta neighborhood.

"I'm never going to do that again," he said, after they stopped along the curb in front of their house. There were muddy grooves in the lawn.

"What'd that maple ever do to you?" she said. He simply stared in its direction. "How fast were you going?"

"I guess I wanted to shake it a little."

"After they took you away, I backed the car off the lawn," she said. "Kind of surprised the thing is running."

"They say it's a good car," he said in an absent way. "I'm going to sit out here for a minute, all right?"

She left him there. He watched her shut the front door, then hung his head, and when he looked up again, he considered the other houses in the neighborhood. He imagined going over to each one, knocking on the door, trying to explain. Instead, he got on his smartphone and looked up numbers for North Georgia landscapers. Chet would never pledge to give up drinking. But when he wanted to go out, he could at least ask someone to pick him up. Or he could take a taxi.

Chet had any number of friends to drink with; he and Tom Borchardt already went out together about once a month. Tom would only have a couple of beers. It was all he wanted, and he knew how to make them last. Tom was Chet's age and a manager at the Ingles store just after the I-285 off-ramp. Chet imagined that Tom, like any number of his buddies, had a thing for Donna. Tom liked to tease Chet, ask him things like, *How'd the old catahoula get something like that?*

Chet could've confessed, *It's not like you think.* But he'd rather make Tom laugh. Once Chet said, "I'm Jack Lemmon to her. *JFK* Jack Lemmon, not *Save the Tiger* Jack Lemmon. One day I'll just be a lemon in her hand."

"Lucky you," Tom had said.

A few months after the lawn incident, in the middle of August, Chet and Tom went out together and sat in the Primrose. Tom had to be at work at eight the next morning and had one Heineken and then half of another one, while Chet knocked back several gin and tonics. Tom drove him home. He said, "Hey, I think somebody left you something." Outside the front door it looked like someone had left a plastic grocery sack. "Must be nice, all these good things waiting for you," Tom said. Chet waved at him. After stumbling to the door, he picked up the sack and then went inside. He peered into the bag and found a cakebox. Shaking his head, he stuck everything in the refrigerator and ambled down the hall.

At sunrise, Chet emerged from his bedroom and went to the kitchen. Somewhere, Donna had music playing. They slept in different rooms; insomnia for each of them was worse when they'd shared a bedroom. Chet made coffee, and once it began to brew, he opened the refrigerator door. He saw the plastic sack with the cake-

box and wondered if it was from a neighbor, maybe to commemo-
rate...something. A thanks for not running over their children.
Those fucking neighbors, he thought.

He set the box on the counter and opened it to find a man's
dress shoe with a scuffed toe and a worn leather sole. The pad inside the shoe had curled; even though it had been refrigerated, the
shoe had a musty smell.

The shoe seemed like an ominous sign, but he couldn't explain it. What was it doing in a cakebox? He wondered if he ought
to be frightened. His mind racing, he put it all on the floor and
stepped back. He tried to think of anyone who might have left him
such a thing, perhaps as a wonderful, coded message. *I still have the
other one...you forgot them...when you spent the night with me. That
night of magic.* He wanted to smile at this. *No,* he thought. *That
wouldn't be it.* It wasn't his shoe, anyway.

Leaving the shoe behind, he stepped into the rec room carrying two mugs of coffee. The house had been built in the '60s, and
the previous owner had put a bar in one corner of the room. Lino-
leum counter, three stools. On the counter, Donna's CD-radio
played "Ave Mary A" by Pink. Though he liked the song, Chet
halved the volume. He set a mug next to the player, looked over to
the two solid white mannequins positioned in the center of the
room. Donna used one male, one female for her eBay store. The
male wore gray shorts, no shirt. The female had on an orange, one-
piece swimsuit. White visors rested on the crowns of their heads.
He walked closer to the window that gave a view of the backyard,
saw her standing in the grass, having a smoke, looking out to the
houses in Clement Circle. The development held houses with
lawns, handsome young trees. Sugar maples, live oaks, Chinese
elms.

Chet and Donna had met three years ago, when she was
thirty-five years old, at City Club Marietta golf course. She hung

around the clubhouse, rounded out foursomes. The club pro didn't mind; she was pretty, even helped pour drinks at the bar. She nodded and smiled to Chet whenever their paths crossed. The first time he asked her to join him for a round, she immediately accepted. During their round, each tried to let the other win and it took forever. They began to date and he picked up the checks and, after a while, she stopped protesting. He invited her to live with him; she said she'd need a week to think about it, but then called to accept a couple of days later. He promised life would be easy and simple and they wouldn't place a lot of expectations on one another.

Not long after she moved in, his stock portfolio nosedived. The portfolio had been built from an inheritance left to him by his mother, who'd had three husbands all told. When the news came, he made himself a stiff drink and went to tell Donna, who was sitting up in bed, reading. He sat on the edge of the bed and tried to make light of things. He said that if the stocks took another hit like that, they both would have to get jobs. He grinned at this; her expression stayed stony. He knew enough about her. What happened to Chet's investments was not an unfamiliar story to Donna. She'd grown up around money, gone to good schools, done some traveling. Then one day her mother called and said Donna's father had just been arrested for mail fraud and tax evasion. While her father did a year and a half in a medium-security prison, Donna married a wealthy, middle-aged lawyer who'd been chasing her for years. He cheated on her, and after she left him, she married another man and cheated on him. When she moved in with Chet, she wanted them each to take a pledge of fidelity. "Sure," he'd said. "Of course."

He sat on the sofa, listened to another song by Pink, felt like switching to radio, something less challenging—a call-in sports show. He heard Donna cough on the other side of the door, and when she opened it she said, "Oh." He nodded in the direction of the coffee mug on the bar counter. She was barefoot this morning, wore black jeans, a brown-and-blue-striped T-shirt. Mug in hand, she sat down on the sofa, a few feet from him. Chet could smell the smoke on her. Beyond the mannequins, the rec room window let in lemon-colored sunlight.

After a minute, he said, "Somebody left a shoe in a box on our doorstep."

"A shoe...right, my mother," she said. "She called yesterday. I told you about it." She hadn't but he didn't say anything. "She wants me to find a certain pair for my father...wants to surprise him. She thinks they might not make them anymore...these Florsheim wingtips he used to wear. She tried to explain to me what they looked like. But it frustrated her somehow. We decided it would be simpler if she just dropped them off." Donna shrugged. "I guess one tells you plenty."

"I thought maybe somebody had a message for me," Chet said. "One of the neighbors." He thought she might ask what time he'd gotten in last night, but they sat in the quiet, sipping. He'd gone to bed without checking on her. He didn't knock on her door when he'd been drinking; they had a rule about that.

"I don't know what they could tell you," she said.

"So she wants to buy him an old pair of shoes?"

"Not old. Just better condition than what he has. She wants to get a deal. Of course, she didn't say that. Those had to cost two-fifty a throw back in the day. She wants to get him going again. Get him back out there. Legally or otherwise."

"A pair of Florsheims usually don't hold that kind of power."

"She wants to tell herself she's trying to get him going. That's what I think, anyway."

They drank their coffee while the CD played. "Where're they headed?" He gestured in the direction of the mannequins.

"Why, paradise," she said. "The clothes anyway. Those mannequins stay with me."

"Well, they have to make a living."

"Where'd you put that shoe?" she said.

"Kitchen floor."

She left the rec room, and in a moment he heard water running in the kitchen sink. He imagined Donna's mother, Audra Britt, carrying the sack to the door, leaving it there without knocking, then walking back to the curb, getting in her car and driving away. She didn't approve of Chet and Donna together, though she would never say as much aloud, certainly not to Donna.

Chet had tried to imagine Donna's reaction to the news that the family fortune was lost and her father was headed for jail. She'd told Chet a little about it. He knew she'd hollered at her mother, "What will I do now? What can I count on?" Donna regretted it, said she was as ashamed of that as she was of her father for cheating investors, some of whom were probably working class.

Not long after Chet told her about his falling stocks, she started an eBay business. A couple times a week, she drove the Lexus to secondhand stores as well as the Salvation Army. She found other stores all the way over in Clarke County. At first, she took cellphone photos of the clothes she bought and posted them on her seller's page. He offered to buy her a digital camera, and eventually they went in halves. Donna laid out a pair of pants or a sweater vest on the kitchen table and took photos. She listed the sizes, along with condition (*like new; worn at the cuffs*). Sales, at first, were slow. She decided the clothes needed to be modeled, though she didn't think it was a good idea for him or her to do it—even if the clothes fit. She would hold up a sky-blue blouse, pull the sleeves out with her arms, tuck her chin on the neckline. *For a better built woman than me*, she'd write. *Look at the beautiful color!* He held up items, too: a black blazer, a madras shirt, khaki pants. *Nice for casual times,* she'd write. *Some wear.* Sales improved. Donna purchased the mannequins from a department store going out of business. Those helped. It seemed as if she was selling everything she brought in. She kept the mannequins in the rec room, liked to use the natural light from the windows. She usually took her photos when the sun was rising or setting.

He remained on the sofa, listened to the footsteps in the kitchen. It sounded like she was limping. One quiet step then a heavier one. What was she doing, wearing the shoe? He squinted at the sunlight. He thought, *She works at this. She's solving things. She won't need anyone to support her.* He felt sweat on the back of his neck. He didn't love her, probably never had. He was going to die a despondent old man, but while she was here it still felt like he had a chance at something. He told himself, *I worked, too, once. I worked at a lot of things when I was coming up. I didn't love it but I liked it. I shined my shoes every night. I am not the man I was. What man can say that, Donna? I've tried to take things more easily, enjoy my time.* He felt drained, out of energy. But he knew she disliked his jumbled, needy, hangover talk.

He walked out to the kitchen, found her seated at the table. On the floor, near her bare feet, the shoe was outside the box. She shrugged and said, "I get it. I know this type of shoe. I'm getting all these flashbacks right now. When I was a kid, he slapped on the Aqua Velva. Then, at some point, he moved on to CK."

What did he wear in medium security? Chet thought it, knew better than to speak it. He understood that she was already annoyed with him. He thought about saying, *Maybe you can order me a pair.* Instead, he sat at the table and said, "Listen, I want to talk to you."

She looked thoughtful.

"I'm going to quit drinking," he said.

She watched him and her expression wasn't unkind.

He said, "I am. Starting today. I just...it's just time to stop. I'm tired of feeling this way, you know?"

"It would be better for you if you quit."

"I just want to be somebody else. Someone a little different." She regarded him patiently. "What?" he said. "I've been thinking about this. It didn't just hit me." His mug was on the table. His arms were on either side of it, his hands in loose fists. "Goddamnit," he said.

"What are you going to do today, Chet? Who's making breakfast?"

"Just talk to me for a minute, okay?"

"All right."

He exhaled. "I'm sorry. That shoe, it got under my skin or something. Your mom is messing with me."

"Right. She knew you'd come home drunk, find the shoe, flip out."

He considered not saying anything else. He didn't look at her when he said, "She put a shoe in a cakebox. She's telling us something." He eyed his mug, shook his head. "I'm gonna take the Lexus out, have the guy look at it. It was gasping a little the other day."

"I can do it. I wanna take this shoe back. I guess I don't see them enough. They only live across town. It's not like I'm mad at them." He waited for her to add, *Anymore.*

"The mechanic flirts with you," Chet said. "He did that last time and I was right there with you. He won't pay attention."

"Maybe he'll do a better job if it's only me."

"We ought to go together. We ought to do more things together."

"Go to see a mechanic?"

"No. We could ride out to your parents' house together."

She tilted her head. "Why?"

"Just because."

"You and me, it makes my mother uncomfortable. It's who she is."

"Your father won't mind."

"My father is okay with everything now. That's sort of the problem, Chet. At least as she sees it. I think I'm begin—"

"I want to go out there with you."

Her faint eyebrows narrowed. "No. You are just having one of...your days. I'm not in the mood for drama. I don't want to sit around and listen to you and my parents try to get to know one another."

"Well, I'm going, okay?"

In a moment, she said, "Fuck it." She leaned down, stuck the shoe in the cakebox, closed the lid, set it on the table and shoved it in his direction. He caught it before the box knocked over his mug. "Take it," she said. "I'm not riding with you. Don't bother me again today, either." She stood, left the room. He heard her steps, a door close. In a moment he stood too, picked up the box and went to the front door. Beyond the sugar maple, the Lexus sat in the driveway. The landscaper had been of the opinion that the car crash hadn't hurt the tree at all. The leaves would turn their beautiful sweet-potato color in the fall. They were olive with summer now, swaying in the warm breeze. He walked a quarter-moon path around the tree to get to his car.

He backed out onto the street, put the Lexus in drive. The box rode in the passenger seat. At a stop sign, he looked over at it, said, "Go to hell," then went ahead. At the next stop sign, he glanced at the box again. The Lexus sputtered, leveled out. The mechanic's shop wasn't far, a mile and a half, and when he got there he saw a car occupying each space in the garage's three bays. Chet parked next to a tow truck and made his way for the office, the waiting room. He flipped through the pages of a car-buying guide. On the TV on the shelf above the cash register, a reality-court judge seemed angry about something.

"What seems to be the problem?" a voice said.

Chet turned, nodded to the mechanic who owned the shop. Ben was his name. He had big hands, pale arms. Thin hair on top. He smiled at Chet. "Just seems to be missing...the engine," Chet said.

"I can check," Ben said. "In about an hour. You can wait or you can come back."

"Lemme think about it."

Ben kept smiling.

Chet said, "She's not with me today."

"Huh?" Ben said.

Chet watched him. "I'll come back, okay?"

"Suit yourself."

Chet pulled off the lot faster than he should've, waved in the rear view to the car he'd cut off, didn't check to see the driver's reaction. The smell of motor oil lingered in his nostrils. At a stoplight, he thought about how he had once dressed for work, the aftershave he'd used. He'd been married before; he and his wife had both worked at office jobs. They'd had a good love life, for a while. He looked to the cakebox, imagined he should have taken the inheritance and started his own company. *What could I have come up with? I just know how to show up.* He exhaled, felt his shoulders sag, heard a car horn behind him, and pulled ahead.

The Ingles Tom Borchardt managed sat right off I-285, which was nobody's friend. Traffic on Justice Lane turtled along; the cakebox bothered him. The store's lot was half full, and after he pulled into a parking slip, he considered stuffing the box into a trash can near the store entrance. He left it where it was, walked toward the store with his hands in his pockets. The air felt cool inside, and he went to the cigarette counter, asked the female clerk there if she could knock on the door to Tom's office, which was adjacent to a display of by-the-carton Marlboros. When the door opened, she pointed with her thumb and Tom looked in Chet's direction. Chet said, "Coffee?" Tom held up five fingers.

Chet couldn't think of what he needed, but he walked up and down aisles in the store. Then he made his way over to the bakery, where he ordered a coffee and a chocolate donut. He took a place at a booth for two in the little cafe there. On the wall above him were framed studio shots of past Employee of the Month winners. He considered the expressions of the people in the photos. Then, without a word, Tom slid in across from him. He held a can of soda and wore a white button-down shirt with a maroon necktie. The shirt was small on him. Tom's soft-looking gray hair was combed to one side, his mustache neatly trimmed. The thumb-print-sized faint patches of broken blood vessels under each of his eye sockets looked prominent in the bright light of the store.

Tom popped the lid on his soda. "Hell, I thought you'd sleep till noon."

"I guess I have stuff on my mind."

"Who brought you the dinner last night?"

Chet had a bite of donut in his mouth. After he swallowed, he said, "It was...a shoe. Something for Donna's eBay store. That's the way it is around our place. Half-dressed mannequins. The odd shoe. I want to ask you something. No bullshitting around. If I need a job, will you give me one here? Can I get something like that?"

Tom frequently looked amused at what Chet had to say. He brought the soda to his mouth, said, "What kinda work are you thinking about?"

"I could wear a shirt and tie like you do. No problem."

"Managers and assistant managers wear those."

"I could go open collar. I could stock shelves. Absolutely. I am seriously asking you this."

"Stocking shelves is where everybody starts."

"What color shirt do I wear for that?"

"Light green."

Chet drew in a long breath, let it out. "All right. Okay." His voice was quieter. "Stock boy. Where do I apply? I mean, is there an application form?" He took a sip of coffee. His hand seemed to be trembling. "How long did it take for you to get where you are?"

"Four years to make assistant manager. And that's when this chain was doing really well."

"I'm a quick study. When I have to be."

"It's about stamina." Tom had an elbow on the table, and the side of his face rested against his palm. "The official application is just...paper." His eyes moved out to the store floor. He watched customers, employees. "Is this about your girlfriend?" Tom said. "If she wasn't living with you, would you be wondering about a job?"

Chet felt indignant, yet he couldn't find anything to say. "I don't know," he said. "Is that something you ask applicants?"

"I'm asking that as your friend."

"Right." Chet's mouth felt dry. Beyond the restaurant area was an endcap display of chicory coffee. "Stock boy," he said. "I can't imagine her liking that. Maybe she'll see she needs to work harder, too. Maybe we can see if we actually have something in common." His eyes went to Tom. He felt like adding, *There. Okay?*

Tom said, "Hey, we're having a sale on catfish today. Big sale. We've got the catfish market cornered back there. You like catfish, buy a few pounds."

"Sure."

"We had a chance to order so much and get a big discount from a farm outside Meridian, Mississippi. Went a little overboard. So we'll all be eating it for a while. On toast, atop our spaghetti."

His voice turned quiet. "You're funny, you know. You're full of shit, but you're funny."

"I'm not kidding you about working here."

"Say the word, I'll put you on."

"Thank you." Chet nodded, exhaled.

"Any time."

Chet said, "I'm going to buy that catfish now."

"Aisle seven, straight back."

Chet dropped his napkin and coffee cup into a trashcan, went down aisle seven, and asked for three pounds of catfish. The young woman working behind the counter wore a hair net, had fingernails painted bright blue. The wrapped fish felt heavy in his hand, and he asked if she could pack ice around it. She used a clear plastic bag for this. Chet picked out a pack of mints as he waited in line to check out. He paid for everything, then stepped out into the morning sunshine. When he reached the car, he set the bag on the floorboard of the passenger side. He drove toward the mechanic's shop. "All right, a job," he said, his voice soft. He cut his eyes in the direction of the box that held the shoe and said, "Stick that in your pipe."

He sat in the waiting area while his car went up on the hydraulic lift in the garage. Someone had changed the channel to CNN. The sound was low and he watched with faint interest. From the garage, it sounded as if somebody was pounding on a metal pipe with a wrench, then the sound ceased. Laughter echoed. Chet had chosen not to work after getting his inheritance; part of this was because he was a normal human being who wanted an easy, good life, and there was also the hope that a lot of free time would somehow produce a more fascinating, passion-filled existence. He couldn't say that had been the case. He thought of Donna, what he had first hoped for when she moved in. Chet had learned some things through his only marriage. He and his wife had placed a lot of pressure on one another. They panicked when they were not happy; they worried they were not right for one another. He could not help thinking of Donna's parents, each with white hair already. Of course, they weren't going to think much of him, an older man taking in their daughter, someone they had cared for so tenderly. She was an object to Chet, a suggestion that his own aging process was not absolute, that he still could feel like a vital man. He tried to imagine himself as an eighty-year-old, stooped forward, his shaking hands stocking shelves.

He had already more or less decided he wouldn't be taking the shoe over to the house of Donna's parents today. These people were strangers to him; the attempts at socializing were always stiff and morose. At one of their rare get-togethers, Chet and Donna's father had sat in lawn chairs in Chet's backyard. The men were drinking beers and the women were inside. Chet thought it would be all right to ask, so he said, "Can you tell me about prison?"

There'd been a pause. Chet was fairly certain he'd offended the guy and didn't say anything else. "Medium security," was the first thing Donna's father said. Then, "I received a lot of advice before I went in. I was told to have all my dental work done, get a thorough physical. The idea was medical care at medium security wouldn't be so good. I found it to be decent, actually. The staff was quite kind."

Chet would've been interested for him to say more, but he didn't.

"All ready." Ben the mechanic stepped into the waiting area while rubbing his hands into an oily-looking rag. "Fuel line. I got the damages here." At the cash register, Chet held over a credit card before Ben showed him the bill. After handing Chet his receipt, Ben pulled Chet's car out to the lot, then got out and walked straight for the garage. Chet guessed this might have been because the inside smelled like catfish, though actually it didn't. There was still plenty of ice left in the plastic sack. If anything, the inside of the car smelled like gas and oil. Chet headed for his neighborhood, understood the effects from his hangover were gone. He thought about a cold beer.

In the house, he put the catfish away, then walked down the hall toward Donna's bedroom and knocked on her door, which was already open a crack. He stuck his head inside; she leaned back against the headboard of her bed, the laptop balanced on her thighs. He took a step into the room, waited for her to object. When she didn't, he sat on the edge of the bed, an arm's length from her bare feet. "I didn't go to your parents' house," he said. "I went to Ingles, applied for a job. I want to work. I want to be like you, working on something." He faced a bureau as he spoke.

"What am I working on?" she said.

"Your store. Dressing the mannequins. The shoe..."

"The shoe?"

"I see you're figuring things out, Donna. You want a full life. I'm happy for you."

"I'm not figuring out anything. What are you talking about?" He turned to her. She said, "What would you do exactly at the Ingles, Chet?"

"I don't know. Start at the bottom. Stock shelves."

"Are we broke? Tell me. Are we broke?"

"No."

"You're having a very strange day today."

"What's wrong with applying for a job?"

"Are you telling me you want me to leave? Just say it, then. Be a man about it."

"That's not what I am saying."

"I am not working, okay?" she said. "I'm playing around, I'm dressing mannequins in used clothes. You're seeing things that aren't there."

"What's wrong with working? I don't think I understand."

"I don't work, okay? That's not how I want to live my life."

"What you're saying…it doesn't sound good, Donna."

"I don't care how it sounds. I want to be taken care of. I have interests. I make a little money with my store. I don't want the pressure of owning a business. Come on. You've been on the wrong side of things all day. Do you want me to leave? You didn't answer my question."

"No," he said, right away.

"You want to work, work," she said. "I don't need to be dragged into that. What are you going to do, wear a uniform?" He didn't answer. "You didn't grow up rich, Chet. You don't know what that's like. You lucked into some money and you live easy. We live easy here. Even if this is less than what I'm used to. I'm not complaining, though, all right? I know what I've got. My little store is pretty cool. I don't mind sifting through bins of used clothes. I like to think about lives other people have. I'm not a snob. I don't mind going to secondhand stores at all. I think about people struggling and then I feel fortunate. Because I know I am not going to struggle. I'm not going to do that. That isn't me. What kind of work would you do at the Ingles? What would you be in charge of?"

"Nothing," he said. "I haven't applied yet. Not officially." He paused. "I don't want you to leave, Donna. I was afraid of that this morning." His voice turned quiet. "I'm not broke." He didn't say anything else.

"It wasn't easy growing up rich," she said. "We had a colonial-style house, three stories, in Virginia Highlands. Our unhappiness was different than it is now. We all just kept asking for things and getting them."

"You've mentioned that, I think."

"My parents...well. I'm trying to hold on to something here. Men my age don't understand. They want, they want too much."

"All right," he said. "Jesus."

"At this point, I just want to start this day all over again," she said. He nodded without looking at her. "Hey," she said. "I'm not leaving, okay? And you're not asking me to?" He shook his head again. He understood he was not going to feel any better today. It was just one of those days where that wasn't going to happen.

"The box with the shoe is in the passenger seat," he said. He thought about the next time he'd go drinking with Tom—even though he'd told Donna this morning he wanted to quit drinking. She hadn't believed it, that was the main thing. When he went out with Tom, he wondered which of them would bring up the subject of working at Ingles first. Of course, Chet had lost interest in the idea by now. He figured Tom wouldn't bring it up because they were drinking buddies and they liked it that way. "I bought catfish for dinner, a whole lot of catfish," he said.

"Not my favorite," Donna said. "But I can go online to look for the best ways to serve it." Her voice found some energy.

"Okay," he said.

"I can print some ideas for you. That okay?"

He said, "Did you find a match for the shoe? The ones your father used to wear?"

She considered his face. "I'll be able to find something close to it. Bring it back in, will you?"

He sat on the edge of the bed for a minute longer. He pictured the worn shoe on the kitchen table, the two of them looking at it, not speaking, but thinking the same thing.

"I'll put it in the rec room," Chet said, getting to his feet. When he closed the door, he did so quietly. He went to the front door, stepped outside, and looked up to the canopy of the maple. He heard the leaves rustling. He stood still, in the shade provided by the tree. He reminded himself of how beautiful it would be in the Fall.

Valdosta

I once worked as a pari-mutuel clerk at a dog track in Shorter, Alabama. People handed over their money, and I punched out betting tickets. I didn't mind being around all those trays of cash, though I knew the gamblers were going at it the wrong way: you couldn't beat the dogs. Out of the blue one morning, the general manager of the track phoned me at home, said his race caller had quit on him. The general manager told me there'd be a little boost in pay if I'd take over that gig. I would need to begin immediately; the matinee card started in a couple of hours. The general manager sensed my objection because he said, "It's not a real high-skilled job, Wayne. Put on the headset, say the numbers of the dogs in the order they're running, identify the winner."

So I did it. And for one fall season, that was my voice that could be heard from the VictoryLand dog track's PA system. "There they go. That's the two in front, the seven is chasing after it. They're followed by the eight, the four, and the one..." I felt like doing more with the calls, jazzing them up some. I started using the names of the dogs. "Here comes Honey Blonde down the stretch in front...Lucky Strike is trying to catch her...but he won't..." I called the races accurately, but the players griped. The general manager summoned me to his office. "These bettors play numbers," he said. "They have lucky numbers. They've got it down to that, so let's make them happy. You call numbers, not the names of dogs, okay?"

I'd been calling the races for a few months when the track was shut down and the owner and general manager were indicted for money laundering. While he was out on bond, the general manager took the time to e-mail, wish me luck. He mentioned Big T

Wholesalers, an outfit in Valdosta, Georgia, that was run by a cousin of his. They warehoused salvage-store junk, leftovers. A hundred cases of Romney's BELIEVE IN AMERICA T-shirts; a thousand unopened sets of year-old Super Bowl shot glasses. He said they were always looking for a good salesman. I could not recall mentioning to him or anyone else that I wanted to be in sales; maybe he was simply trying to help me out. Anyway, I wasn't long on options at the time and sent over a one-page resume to Big T. The next day my phone rang; a week later I'd moved to Valdosta.

I'd been living there for a few months when I met Glennis McCarty, and a few months after that she moved in with me. We were married in a JOP ceremony in New Orleans. We spent our three-day honeymoon hanging out in the French Quarter; it was her second marriage and my first. We read in the *Times-Picayune* that Brad and Angelina were in town, and Glennis said she'd do anything for me if she could have her photo taken with them. That didn't happen, but we blew out a Visa card on the trip. Back in Valdosta, we'd been talking about buying a house, but we put that on hold for a while. We wound up living in the same apartment for a couple more years. She worked at the university, in the administration office, and took a class every once in a while. She was a pretty lady with long brown hair and shimmering blue-green eyes. She wore makeup she didn't need, though it just wasn't a good idea to try and talk to her about that.

One day the owner of Big T, Jeffrey Mallet, brought packages to the office, said he had one for each member of the sales team. There was Maureen, Rudy, and myself. Jeffrey was a big man with a wide face and swept-back gray hair. I noticed he bore a resemblance to the dog-track general manager. "Just got six thousand of these units," he said, "for a laugh." He placed one on my desk. The cover of the cardboard box said, DISASTER KIT. He didn't visit the sales office often, and I tried to look appreciative. The package in front of me was the size of three stacked pizza boxes. Inside was a folded-up, cellophane-thin blanket made of a shiny, foil-like material. A medical kit, a blue plastic case with a Red Cross symbol, came with it. I brought out the blanket. Maureen was on her feet, already had one draped over her shoulders. The blanket crinkled as she walked around her desk; it reached all the way to the office's dark industrial carpet.

"Miss Plutonium, twenty twenty-one," Rudy said.

"Nice," Jeffrey said. "Actually, you're not far off."

When I brought my box home that evening and showed it to Glennis, she seemed interested in the medical kit. There were Band-Aids, an ACE bandage, a bag of cotton balls, a bottle of aspirin. The kit also held a paperback titled *Be Prepared*. She thumbed through the pages.

"This material is dated," she said. "I don't see anything about live shooters. We have guidelines on campus for that."

"You told me."

"Of course, we're supposed to memorize those. One is, 'Don't leave the building. Lock yourself in, stay down.' Fuck that, I'm not cowering in some classroom."

"I'm with you," I said.

"Sweetheart," she said. "Why is this here? On my table?"

"There's a chance for each of us to make three hundred bucks," I said.

She exhaled. Her eyes went to the coffee mug in front of her. We'd finished dinner a while earlier. When she looked my way again, she said, "Go ahead."

"We're going to sell these things at retail stores. Jeffrey knows they need a little something extra."

"Well, they do."

"Packaging."

"Ah," she said.

"He wants to dress up the boxes. He wants the cover of the box to have images, people wearing the blankets. Models."

"Professional models."

"He doesn't want to pay those prices. And they want the people wearing the blankets to look like regular people. The graphics guys will digitally fill in the disaster in the background. A burning house or an explosion."

"And...I'm the regular person you seek?"

"You know what I mean."

"I'd face the camera, looking all-come-fuck-me in my elegant foil blanket?"

"I'll be right there next to you. I already volunteered. Jeffrey mentioned that we would be looking more away from the camera, in the direction of a disaster, and pointing. I think Rudy is going to do a cover, too."

"What about Maureen?"

"No."

"Good-bye, black lesbian demographic."

"The shoot is tomorrow. They want to get these boxes on the shelves. The craziness in Syria, *An Inconvenient Truth*...it's a mess out there." I must've been using my sales voice. She looked at me in a motherly way.

Glennis guided the box away so she could place her arms on the table. She was still dressed from her job. "These boxes will be on display in places...around town?"

"Not Walmart or anything, not that mafia. We can't get our stuff in there."

"Wayne, the university wants its employees to present a certain kind of image."

"I know that." It was a talk we'd had. Last December, I'd decided to make a bet on the SEC title game with a local bookmaker; not long after that the guy got busted. The newspaper said the bookie had an extensive client list, but I knew there was no way the list would ever get published, not in a small town like this one. Glennis had worried about guilt by association, losing her job because of me—even though it was a job she didn't like. "I didn't promise you would do this, Glen," I finally said. "I just told the boss I'd ask. He wants to have two different covers. A man and woman on one. For the other shoot, Rudy's gonna have a kid with him, borrow somebody's." She was sitting back in her chair by now. Her arms were crossed.

"I was pretty enough to be a model," she said. "That's what people said about me when I was younger."

Oh shit, I thought. I said, "I'm going to do it. I don't work for any university. I already told the boss I would. We both do it, it's six hundred bucks." She didn't say anything. Of course, I'd had the chance to think about all of this earlier in the day; it looked like I just hadn't thought of everything. When I was at the office, I always sized up things the way a salesman needed to. We talked our shit and sold our trash. All the salespeople at Big T—Maureen, Rudy, and myself—were pretty slick. Pepa-N-Salt-N-Pepa— Maureen nicknamed us that because she and Rudy were black and I wasn't. "Do you worry it'll be bad luck to pose for something like that?" I said. "Be honest now."

"You're going to continue to try and talk me into this?"

"No."

She still had her arms folded. "I want you to go down on me tonight," she said. Glennis was pretty direct about what she expected to happen in bed, though we didn't usually talk about it at the dinner table. I'd screwed up a little; it wasn't a harsh sentence. She glanced in the direction of the front door. "I don't know if I want to do this," she said. "A disaster girl…"

"Let's put this away," I said, pulling the box closer. I waited for her to pick up the manual and stick it back inside. Then I closed the lid. I got up from the table and carried the box over to the closet by the front door.

After that, Glennis decided to take her laptop to the bedroom. She closed the door partway. Later, when I tapped on the door, I had a glass of wine for her. I pushed the door back, saw that she wore her black pajamas. Then I went to the kitchen, pulled down the bottle of Dewar's, and made a Scotch and water. I sat on the couch in our little living room area. I always liked to think about who I might be making a pitch to the next day. In sales, preparation was oxygen, and getting caught off guard by anything was practically a mortal sin. I took out my iPhone, texted a message to the number I had for Jeffrey. "Better find someone else to play my wife tomorrow." I thought about not sending it, but then I did. I wondered who he would come up with. I took off my shoes, finished my drink. When I pushed back the door to the bedroom, Glennis was nude from the waist down. She was still sitting up in bed, laptop on her knees. She glanced at me, then to her laptop. "Ready?" she said.

I didn't know what she had been looking at on the Internet, but she was ready. Once we got going, she kept talking. "Stay down there, stay down there." Afterward, after everybody was in good shape, we lay together in bed with the lights on. She could also be pretty graphic with the sex talk; once she said my sperm left her with an aftertaste like chlorine. But she was quick to add, "That's not your fault, sweetheart. I mean, God knows what they're putting in our bodies anymore." I knew I wasn't going to be getting a lot of head in this marriage, that's what it amounted to. Maybe that should've mattered more. Anyway, this time, she said, "They let the Georgia football coach sell pickup trucks. He's on billboards. It's not like I would be advocating disaster… Honestly, I'd like to get out there a little bit. Let people get a look at me."

I could have taken the discussion in any number of ways then, and I thought about bringing up the subject of makeup; they probably wouldn't want her to get all dolled up for the shoot. We'd need to look natural, like something terrible was happening. *Disasters hit fast.* That might be her answer. *You're living your life, you're all dressed up for something...then boom.* I wanted to say something about going to New Orleans, that we had an anniversary coming up and that we ought to go over there and have a great time, no matter what we made from the photo shoot. She said, "Get the light, will you, please?" I did this, and then she said, "Good night."

"Good night."

I lay up in bed for a while after that and thought a little more about who Jeffrey could get for my wife. Probably a niece of his or his secretary's daughter. He was like that, always just throwing shit together. Having an elaborate plan meant missing the chance that popped up right in front of you. The guy knew his world, I'll give him that. No one in Pepa-N-Salt-N-Pepa worried about his company going under.

When I fell asleep that night, I didn't have any dreams about ISIS, me on my knees, a guy in a black hood standing at my shoulder. My dreams weren't like that; they weren't even like Dali paintings with melting clocks or elephants walking on stilts. When I was a teenager in Kentucky I worked on a horse farm, and I still dreamed about that. In the dream, I carried buckets across a green field that went on and on. I held the metal handles and could feel the weight of the water. I could hear the sound of my own feet moving through the high grass. I took this dream to mean I might not have the greatest imagination in the world, but I was steady and I was strong. Anyway, what I dreamed about was not what I dreamed of, and I knew the difference.

Glennis got out of bed before I did the next morning. I felt her rise and heard her steps going for the door. She'd pulled on her pajama bottoms. Out in the living room, I heard a door open and associated the rest of the sounds with her taking the disaster kit from the closet. I heard a rustling, pictured her walking about with the blanket of foil wrapped around her. We didn't have any mirrors out there, so she might've been looking at her reflection in the window. In a little while, I smelled bacon cooking, and when I went to see about things Glennis had breakfast ready. She'd put the box away. I sat across from her, took a sip of coffee. I'd put some points on the board for her last night, that was one thought I had. She was usually preparing for work around this time. She said, "Maybe I'll do the thing, the shoot or whatever, with you today. I'm going to call in, take a half day. I can't remember the last time I've done that."

"Great," I said.

"What time should I be there?" she said.

"Well, we're gonna do it first thing this morning. I think in the conference room. Glen, I need to tell you something."

"All right."

"I had to text Jeffrey last night, tell him we might need another woman for the shoot. You weren't sure. He'll understand that you changed your mind. People do that, but he needs to get this done. So we need to get ready. Be ready."

"You couldn't have waited?"

"Yeah, I could've. But if it's not you, I have to have somebody else."

"You guys can just use Maureen."

"I already told you about that. Besides, that would be interracial. You know my route. We'll try to teach everyone a lesson next year, okay? Look, I want you with me. I already told you this yesterday. But if you'd like to do it, let's go on and get there first. I know Jeffrey."

"We're having this nice breakfast here. Look at this." She waved her hand over the table. "If I'm going to be part of the shoot, they can do it when I'm ready. This isn't some...dog race. No offense."

"None taken." Glennis hadn't been with me when I'd had that race-calling job in Alabama. But when we first dated, I did race calls for her, just imagined the greyhounds running right in front of me. Instead of numbers, I'd use names like Mercury Al and Speedy Coyote, wanting to make it something more than just a dog race. She'd smile and shake her head as if there was some part of me that just couldn't be helped.

"We're the stars this morning," she said. "We can make them wait a little."

In front of me was a plate of pancakes, a side of bacon, and a glass of juice, just like at a restaurant. "I know," I said. "Sure."

"What are you going to wear?"

"I have to make a sales call after the shoot. Southern Thrift. A button-down shirt or a polo. I don't think it matters, do you? For somebody like me." I gave her a smile.

In a moment, she said, "If you think it doesn't."

"What about you?" I shoveled food into my mouth.

"I was actually thinking of going casual. Take a change of clothes for work with me."

I swallowed and said, "I think you ought to just wear those pajamas."

She tilted her head. "Honestly," she said.

"Sex sells," I said.

It wasn't a bad thing to say. I decided to just shut my mouth after that and finish my breakfast. I didn't check my messages until I had the shower running. I stood at the bathroom sink and read the one from Jeffrey that said, "No prob." I showered and dressed pretty quick after that. Glennis was putting away the dishes when I got out there. I wondered if she'd changed her mind again. I placed a hand on the middle of her back, kissed her cheek.

"I'm on my way," she said. "Just a few minutes behind you."

On the drive to work, I listened to the news from NPR. I always tried to keep up with things, but my mind drifted. Bad stuff was going to happen, but it didn't mean life was tragic or even unmanageable. If anything, the truth was closer to the opposite of that. The opportunities were out there for the people who didn't let their hearts get fractured by every little thing.

The Big T warehouse sat on the west side of Valdosta, on an empty stretch of Juniper Road, the horizon beyond it dotted with tree clusters and billboards. That morning there were more cars in the lot than usual, even though it was still a few minutes before eight thirty. We were doing the shoot in the conference room, I'd already been told that, but then I passed Rudy in the stairwell and he said the photographer wanted to use the warehouse instead. Something to do with unnatural lighting upstairs. Rudy was in a two-piece suit; he always kept his goatee neat. I caught a whiff of cologne. Best salesman in the county, Jeffrey frequently said. Like a son to me. I dropped my briefcase at my desk, then turned around and headed down the stairs. There was another hallway that led out to the warehouse floor. I opened the door to the warehouse, spotted Rudy. Maureen raised her coffee mug in a toast, though she looked pretty tired. No Glennis.

"There he is," Jeffrey said. "Wayne-man. The Duke!" He stood in front of a portable green screen and appeared cheerful. A photographer tried to get Jeffrey in better focus. Beyond them, forklifts zipped back and forth in the warehouse. As long as it was tuned to classic rock, the warehouse foreman let the guys have a radio. Right then, it played George Harrison's "My Sweet Lord."

Jeffrey stepped in my direction and motioned to a woman standing off to one side to follow. He said, "This is Lorena." The woman was youngish, in her twenties, had black hair pulled tight in a bun behind her head. She wore heels, a turquoise dress. They stopped a few feet from me.

I said, "Glennis is on the way." I shrugged then, felt helpless for a second.

"Hello," Lorena said. She held a purse tight to her hip.

"Hello," I said.

"We're waiting on the kid for Rudy," Jeffrey said. "Y'all go on, go first." He nodded to me. "Your girl gets here, we'll do another one. If there's time." He said, "Let's go!" in the direction of the photographer.

At this point, Lorena and I were left facing one another. We weren't anywhere near the screen. I couldn't help but think of the idea of an arranged marriage. I guessed that kind of thing had its advantages. "Kinda weird, huh?" I said.

"What's that?" she said.

"We're not gonna know what hit us." I pointed with my thumb at the blank screen.

"Oh," she said. She kept her hands folded over her purse. "Right," she smiled.

Jeffrey said, "And somebody give them a couple of those damn covers!"

Maureen moved in the direction of a stack of disaster kits. When Jeffrey had shown up at the sales office yesterday, pitching us on the idea of being models for the tops of the kits, he hadn't asked Maureen until Rudy and I had each agreed to do it. He needed to ask Maureen, but anybody who knew Maureen knew she wasn't going to pose as some guy's wife, not for three minutes and especially not if it involved protection from a disaster. She had a girlfriend named Lisa who everybody thought looked like Erin Burnett. Maureen hadn't made any speech to the boss; I'll pass, she'd said. Jeffrey had said, Of course. Here's some releases for you guys to sign, he'd said to Rudy and me.

Lorena and I arrived near the green screen, where Maureen held out a foil blanket for each of us and then stepped back. Maureen wore her hair short, kept it combed to one side. She had on a beautiful striped dress this morning. Out in the warehouse, someone on a forklift shouted, "Where?"

"All right," said the photographer as he strolled by us. "Pull those things close now, please," he said. He stood at a tripod, took the camera from his neck. "Okay," he said. "Let's go."

Lorena and I were in the spotlights, and I could feel the heat. The foil blanket I had was stiff, like it had been folded in a box for a century. I wanted to ask for a different one.

"That's good, pull them right up to your necks," the photographer said. He stood behind the tripod, had his camera pointed at us. "Okay, look at one another. Miss, you're holding the thing around you like it's a sweater. End of the world now…right on up there. Let's look at one another…try to appear sorrowful." Lorena's expression was the same as it had been a minute ago, guarded. "Good," said the photographer. "Now you, put your hand on her shoulder." I gave her a second to object. When she didn't, I placed my hand over the part of the foil blanket covering her shoulder. "Look at the screen," he said. "Good. Miss, point at the screen, both of you look that way. Super. A few more now…"

A minute later, he said, "Okay, we're done!"

By this time, Lorena and I had our backs to the camera and were holding hands, looking in the direction of the screen. We kept our blankets up with our free hands; I was trying to imagine the end of something on the screen, but I wound up just picturing a sunset. We released our hands, stood back from one another. Somebody applauded, probably Jeffrey. I took the stupid foil blanket away from my shoulders and stepped out of those lights. Rudy's child had arrived, a small boy with a big head of curly hair. Maureen chatted with another woman who must've been the kid's mother, a short woman dressed like she worked in an office somewhere.

"All right, all right," Rudy said when I went over to stand by him. He seemed kind of nervous; usually he'd already be out on his route. Or maybe it was because he had to work with this kid.

Lorena had gone right over to Jeffrey, and he was patting her shoulder now. I learned later that she was his maid. The lady with the kid was a friend of Maureen's from a Pilates class they took together in Little Miami. Jeffrey and Lorena were heading for the door that led to the offices. It was Rudy's turn, his and the little kid's. The little kid seemed playful; his name was Edgar. Once Edgar reached the spotlights, he waved his arms over his head. He did a little dance.

"You go," his mother said. "You show 'em all, boy."

Maureen and the photographer were talking. Rudy and I drew closer to them. The photographer wanted the child to wear one of the blankets. Maureen explained to the photographer that the blankets didn't come in children's sizes, at least not the ones we had to sell. The photographer wondered if one of the blankets couldn't be cut to fit Edgar, but Maureen said this probably would confuse things. A customer might expect a child-size blanket to be in the box. We'd have to note on the box that that wasn't the case. *Protection for children not included.* Was this something we wanted to say? Then there was the question of Rudy wearing a blanket and the kid not wearing one. Wouldn't that make Rudy look…selfish? Somebody wanted to call Jeffrey, but Maureen said not to bother him. Rudy could drape part of his blanket over the child's shoulders.

Once this was agreed upon, Rudy headed for the spotlights, a disaster blanket over his arm. He and Edgar faced the screen and

Rudy leaned down, was ready to hold the blanket to the boy's shoulders. The boy turned quickly in the direction of his mother. She nodded to him; he grinned and waved. "Look ahead, look ahead," she said, her voice soft. Rudy tried to get his attention by gesturing in the direction of the blank screen.

"Maybe a movie will be playing up there," Rudy said. "You like movies?"

At 9:07 A.M., Glennis texted me, said, "Where'm I going?"

I texted back, "Warehouse."

When she arrived on the set, the spotlights near the screen had been shut off. Everyone from the shoot was gone except the photographer. "We finished a little while ago," I said, before she reached my side. She wore faded jeans with ripped-out knees, a black T-shirt. Her hair was loose, fell around her shoulders. I said, "Everybody had to get going." The photographer, kneeling near the tripod, glanced in our direction.

Glennis put her hands in her pockets. For a second, she watched what was happening in the warehouse. "Dirty White Boy" by Foreigner played. "Well, hell," she said. "I tried to look like I needed to be saved from something."

"You look great." To the photographer, I said, "I guess we could turn everything back on, couldn't we? Do a quick shoot with her and me?"

"Need to check with the boss for that," the photographer said. "On a schedule."

By now, the green screen had been packed away. Glennis seemed to be thinking about it.

She turned to the photographer, said, "Can I see what you guys did?"

He stood up in a measured way, wiped his hands together. "Yeah," he said. He removed the camera from the tripod and held it at arm's length as Glennis walked over to him. She leaned in. He seemed to be rolling from one photo to the next. "There they are," the photographer said.

She said, "Mm-hmm."

"And then here's the guy with the kid," he said.

"Uh-huh," she said.

The photographer sighed. "I guess that's it."

Glennis said, "What'll be in the background? When you guys are done?"

I remained a few feet from them. "It might be full of fire," I said.

"I heard them talking about a natural disaster, too," the photographer said. "A result of the ozone." He pointed upward.

Glennis nodded her head, though she seemed distant. She might've been picturing herself in the middle of some disaster while wrapped in her shiny blanket. I said, "Can you take a few of her? Don't worry about the backdrop or anything."

Glennis said, "Yeah." Without a word, the photographer began to fidget with the camera. He held it up to eye level. Glennis turned on a nice smile for him right away.

"Look past my shoulder," he said. It didn't take long. Ten seconds, maybe fifteen. Then he brought the camera down again. He held it out, and she stepped over to see how the shots looked. "All right," she said. "Not bad."

"I'll send these along with the others," the photographer said.

"Great," I said.

"Keep the warehouse as the background," she said.

The photographer continued to pack up his things.

She walked back to me.

"I'll tell Jeffrey you showed," I said. "Maybe he'll pay you anyway."

"That's okay. Jesus."

"Let me walk you out. Unless you want to stay. Ride with me to Southern Thrift?"

"I'll leave that to you."

While we went through the hallway I said, "Maybe we'll be able to use your photos for something else. If we're trying to show all the products we warehouse in a commercial." She didn't respond. "Or maybe if we're selling umbrellas or something. We can make it rain a little behind you."

"A little rain would be okay."

Then we were outside, walking in the direction of her plum-colored Acura. She'd been driving this car since before we'd met; it had hundreds of thousands of miles on it. We arrived at the driver's-side door. I could feel the sun already cooking my forehead, my arms. "You could've been on time, you know," I said.

"I wanted to get my look right," she said. I guessed she was trying to sound innocent. She touched the back of her hand to her forehead.

"You didn't want to do it, did you?" I said.

She reached over, straightened my collar. "It didn't feel right, sweetheart. The only reason I showed up at all was that I just don't want you to think I think I'm better than you."

"I don't think that," I said.

"That's not good for a marriage," she said, her voice gentle. I didn't think she was listening to me. She said, "I came down here. I'm a good wife. I dressed for disaster day."

"I'm going to ask Jeffrey about your money."

"Well, maybe you should."

"How did I look in my photos?"

"A little bewildered," she said. "Just right." She smiled like she had for the photographer a few minutes before, maybe not quite as brightly.

"Listen, that woman in the photo. She meant nothing to me."

"Good one," Glennis said. "You're good." She brought up her fists like a boxer. "But be careful who you call 'regular' next time." Her voice turned quiet. "We don't know regular." She lowered her fists so I could see her clear, blue-green eyes. "You get that, right?" In slow motion, she swung her right fist in the direction of my jaw but then she stopped.

"I get it," I said.

Glennis reached for a back pocket of her jeans and produced a set of keys. "I gotta change, get to school." When she looked at me again, she said, "We okay?"

"Yep."

"See you tonight." Glennis pulled open the driver's door. I stepped back, gave her a little more room. She put the Acura in reverse, then in drive, and zipped off the lot. I stood there for a moment after she was gone. We could've passed on the chance to model for the disaster kit and our day could've gone along like it always did. Right then, it was hard to imagine something terrible happening to either of us. I thought of Glennis and me a few decades from now, with our gray hair and sunken faces, and for some reason I pictured us at a greyhound track, the two of us standing on the asphalt apron, and right after the dogs hit the finish of a race she'd say, "Did you have that one? Did you have the winner?"

What would wind up being in the background for my photo? I checked the horizon: blue skies, trees, a bunch of billboards. The graphics guys could figure it out. Anyway, if you weren't trying to sell something, the future could be hard to predict. I tugged at the front of my polo shirt, then headed back inside.

Library

Heath knows that the Atlanta-Fulton Public Library downtown opens at 10 A.M. on Tuesday–Saturday and never one minute earlier, not even when it's raining and there are a dozen-plus citizens waiting to get inside. The building is eight stories, cube shaped, neutral toned. He's read up on the architecture: it's known as Brutalist, taken from the French words *beton brut*, or "raw concrete." Chinese elms line the street outside the entrance. They have minty-looking leaves that swim prettily in the morning breeze.

When he first started showing up at this library, Heath arrived empty handed. Now he carries a notebook like some of the other patrons. He has tried to make journal-type entries, but every time he's started an entry, his own life doesn't seem all that interesting to him. He's never wished to be a writer and that is true now more than ever. He doesn't believe that the other people with notebooks in here are professional writers. Writing in notebooks is just something they've come here to do.

Before patrons enter the library, all backpacks and briefcases are searched for drugs and weapons. The security guard who looks like Lou Rawls circa "You'll Never Find Another Love Like Mine" will see Heath and his notebook and wave him on through. Heath sometimes finds himself on the second floor with the knee-high, four-person tables and even shorter wooden stools. These are situated near the shelves that hold current editions of hard-copy magazines about beauty or health or fitness or the entertainment industry or politics or America or great things to do in an America city or international destinations or international politics. There are signs on every floor that read,

No Eating No Drinking No Sleeping

On one occasion, Heath broke the sleeping rule. He'd been scratching out a sentence in his notebook and then laid his head on his arm for only a moment. There came tapping on the table. A security guard. "Wake up, please."

Heath sat up, cleared his throat. He said, "I was. I'm... awake."

This morning he's not sleeping when his ex-wife, Jackie, sits down across from him at one of the second-floor tables. "Hi, Heath," she says.

"Hello." He has his notebook open in front of him.

"Pretty morning outside."

"Why yes, I think it is."

"I heard you might've lost your job." She speaks in her regular, non-library voice.

"I guess I did." Heath glances at the table to his right; a bald black man wearing eyeglasses sits in silence, reads a newspaper.

Jackie has shoulder-length, shiny blond hair and clear blue eyes. He hasn't seen her in a year. She studies his face. "Marcy Freeman said she sees you standing outside the library waiting for it to open. Every morning. Looking lost."

"I'm waiting for the library to open. How is that lost?" Though he knows better, he speaks in a non-library voice, too.

She nods to the notebook. "What are you doing, scribbling down your last will?"

He's not in love with Jackie anymore. But her presence has changed the rhythm of his heartbeat. "So I was downsized," he says. "That's all, it's done. You have the day off or something?"

"Hardly." She tosses her head. She wears a silky, cerulean blouse. "Just took a break to walk a few blocks. See about this. You appear to be okay, anyway. Marcy made it sound like you were standing around outside, staring off into space."

"I'm not sure I can deny that."

"I've never thought of you as a poet."

"You shouldn't now."

She shakes her head. He turns the notebook back a page, to some stuff he'd written the day before, pushes that in her direction.

A man with a red face and a white beard sits erect in a chair turning the pages of a novel fast. It seems like he's looking for a certain passage. It seems to be of the utmost importance.

A man sits at a table with his head bowed, his fingers to his forehead. There's nothing on the table in front of him.

The sunlight pouring in through the east window this morning is pretty overwhelming.

He says, "Not fancy. I just see something and write it down. A few of the guys in here are furious. Can fill a notebook in an hour. You ought to see them go." He pauses. "You didn't have to come over here and check on me."

She pushes the notebook back to him. "Actually, I did. You have leads on anything? Come on, let's get moving here."

"I don't stay in the library all day. At noon, I ride the train back to Midtown, go to my apartment, get on the Internet, send emails, make calls. I have about two to three rock 'em-sock 'em hours a day. I do all that in the afternoon. In the mornings, you let working people do their things, be productive." He gives a quick smile, one she doesn't return. "When you ask for a favor, always do it later in the day…" He shrugs. "There's research about that."

"Why haven't you called me? I can ask around, too."

"Would you ask me? If the shoe…"

A security guard arrives at their table, smiles, and holds a finger to his lips. He nods in a polite way to Jackie and moves away from the table. She leans forward, says, "This is loud?"

Heath decides to write something:

Jackie doesn't seem to understand the rules of the library.

He holds up the notebook so she can see. She whispers, "Ha ha, motherfucker," then sits back again. Heath sets the notebook in front of him. He writes:

A woman I know sits in the chair across from me.

That blue is her color.

He feels his heart sink. He doesn't show it to her, turns the page.

Then he writes:

Jackie needs to get back to her own office.

He holds the notebook so she can see it. She says, "Okay, sure." Since he's been out of work, there have been moments when he has felt the despair that someone who once worked but now doesn't is bound to feel. When he thinks about the job he once had, he sometimes views it as trivial. With Jackie sitting across from him now, he understands why he had a job. He almost feels like he did when he had a job. While he'd had a job, he wasn't ambitious. Heath isn't philosophical, and with a job came explanations, answers. When Jackie left, some of those went with her. There was a reason his job specifically was downsized. He supposes she can put to-gether a lot of this on her own.

"Things okay with you?" he says, trying to sound offhand.

"What? Yes. Yeah," she says. "Right now, as far as my plans go, I'm ahead of schedule. Don't you worry about it." She glances past his shoulder. Across the floor are the microfiche file cabinets; they are metallic, bright red and bright blue. Maybe the guard is standing in front of those right now, holding a finger to his lips.

"I'll come to see you if the well runs dry," he says.

His expression might've turned syrupy because she appears impatient. "Just don't feel sorry for yourself." It's a familiar accusation.

He nods to the notebook. "I'm not," he says.

"Hooray," she says, teasing, looking a little tired.

They sit without speaking. Her eyes go to the notebook, to the page that has the line about her getting back to her own office. "What am I missing out on?" she says, once again in a normal speaking voice. Judging by her expression, they're both surprised by what she's said. He understands she's not talking about a life with him.

"Well, this, I guess." He isn't talking about himself.

She probably understands as much, is glancing now in the direction of the information desk. "I'll come back here in a week. If you're still here, I'm dragging your ass back to the street."

"Okay," he says.

"I gotta go."

"I know."

"I mean, it's written right there." She points. "Don't get up."

He does, partway. "Jackie."

"Sweetheart," she says. She touches her fingers to her mouth in a blowing-you-a-kiss gesture, though she doesn't pucker her lips.

Then she walks past the other tables, to the top of the staircase, starts down. There's her head and shoulders and then her head and then she's gone. It turns silent. He sits again, flips his notebook back a page.

He wants to write another line but instead he murmurs, "You won't have to drag me." The bald guy glances his way, but he's a regular, too. There can be some muttering to oneself here; security forgives it. Heath thinks of books he and Jackie read in college, tries to recall the title of one in particular, a novel that mystified him at the time. About a salesman in the Industrial Age. Will Jackie remember? If he phones her about such a thing, she'll probably accuse him of wanting to talk about something else.

He thinks of words for a search: *Salesman. Industrial Age. Novel.* To use a PC, he'll need to walk over to the information desk and sign in. The older man behind the counter there is humming something…maybe Cohen's "Hallelujah." Heath signs in and heads for a PC, imagining he has just enough to go on.

Resort Life

Before my old man blew the family's eight Detroit-area dry-cleaning stores on account of his compulsive gambling, we used to travel to some of the best hotels in the country. The Breakers, the Drake, the Ritz. Then, along with everything else, he lost my trust fund, the university savings. We turned into Russian nesting dolls. We moved out of our mansion in Bloomfield Hills to a two-story place on Becker Drive. Then into a ranch house in Normalton. I thought it would be a positive step to get away from him and my mother—who apparently believed acknowledging his betting sprees would create more of a problem than trying to stop them—so I applied to colleges in great hotel cities in the South because you didn't need a fortune to start over there. I was happy to get free of the Michigan weather and wound up attending the University of New Orleans. I put myself through school pushing around laundry carts at the Fairmont, then doing dishes and parking cars at Bienville House. During summers, I waited tables and ran trays for room service at the Grove Park Inn in Asheville, North Carolina. Right after graduation, I started as a registration clerk, then made it to assistant manager at the Blanchard Hotel in downtown Atlanta. When our manager, Billy Carlyle, suffered a heart attack and died right there in his office, I took over his job on an interim basis.

As a manager, I felt at ease, like something had been returned to its rightful place. When I was just twenty-six years old, the EW Corp. in Dallas, which owned the Blanchard as well as a number of other hotels, offered me a breathtaking promotion: executive manager at the Carolinian Hotel, a resort on the North Carolina coast with ninety-one guest rooms.

By this time, my parents were living in a one-bedroom rental apartment in a complex on the west side of Detroit that Inez Hidalgo, a former maid of ours, had recommended to them because of its cleanliness. I visited my parents once, on my mother's fiftieth birthday. There were stacks of newspapers and magazines everywhere. I didn't recognize a single piece of furniture. My father pedaled back and forth on a bicycle to his job at a sandwich shop. He had been going to Gamblers Anonymous for half a dozen years. I brought my mother some sky-blue beach towels with Carolinian logos, items I had purchased at full price from the hotel gift shop. My mother didn't say anything, just hugged me for a minute. She had quit everything, too; smoking, drinking, pills. Predictably, everything that was said between us was dramatic:

> Mother: How do you feel about the world these days, son? Do you look at your life in an optimistic way?

> Me: For heaven's sake, I run a resort. I'm probably the youngest executive manager in the whole country. Do I even need to answer that?

> Father: Your mother and I are living with great humility now. It took a lot for us to finally understand how to do this. Don't let it...I suppose what I am saying, son, is that I am sorry.

> Me: About what?

> Father: We didn't save anything. You'll have to work hard for the rest of your life. I mean, I suppose everyone needs to...

Me: (Suppressing a laugh) I don't work hard. I love my work. Oh, my god.

Mother: It's all right. Your father has been so brave. I didn't know we had this kind of courage inside us.

Me: It's fine. You all didn't ruin my future. Because of you, I simply know what I don't want to be. (A long silence ensues) All right, there had to be a better way to express that. (Silence) I don't hate you. I don't hate anyone.

Mother: It's all right.

Me: I know.

Mother: We're so proud...

Me: Happy birthday.

I hadn't returned. Two Christmases ago, I invited them to stay at the Carolinian, but they gave me all these reasons why they couldn't make it. My mother finally said, "Honey, we just don't live hotel lives anymore." I supposed it would have been strange to see them in the lobby, checking in like two people on holiday. My father had once owned three Cadillacs, a white one and *two* green ones. Now, he just wanted to talk about why the world was such a mysterious place. I certainly didn't tolerate a lot of philosophizing or other forms of messiness from my hotel staff. If one of the maids brought in a squawking baby because the day care was closed, that maid was sent home. A bellhop who argued with his girlfriend on one of the house phones? Suspended. Unkempt uniform? Written up. Bad language? Docked a day's pay. I'd been running the Carolinian for just a few months when I received a call from the home office in Dallas with the explicit order to ease up on the staff. "They're complaining," the company exec said. "It's hard to get any kind of help with what we pay. Half your workers aren't even documented. You know that, right?" The staff also disliked the fact that I was so apologetic to the customers, even though to a good number of our guests, the Carolinian was nothing more than a huge living room. Bare feet on the lobby carpet. Backwards ball caps, shirts hanging out. Arguments. Mothers shouting after their children. In a way, I supposed the customers were the biggest problem of all.

We also had guests like Mrs. Catherine Nance and her son Michael who traveled down from the state of New York for two weeks in May, our shoulder season. They were both slender, blond, and fair. Mrs. Nance was a shade over fifty, I thought. Michael, in his early thirties, didn't appear to have a worry in the world. It was uncanny, the similarity in the shapes of their faces. Once, I stopped by Michael's table at our piano bar, the Meteor Lounge, while he was there having a drink by himself, and he wound up showing me billfold photos of himself and his mother at the Kentucky Derby from two decades earlier. Little Michael wore a child's blazer and his hair was combed back. His mother wore a silky, straw-colored dress, her Derby hat shading the top half of her face. "Look at her," he said. "Thank god, Mother is gorgeous. I imagine I'm not so bad, either, right?" "Of course not," I said. "Where is your mother tonight?" "Upstairs," he said. "I'm bringing her a drink." He raised his glass to me in a toast. "You're a terrific fellow," he said. "I don't know you very well, but I can surely tell that much."

Mrs. Nance's husband spent a lot of time in Tokyo, that seemed to be the story, and Michael, the story further went, was the only company she wanted for her travels. There was the predictable, mean-spirited gossip about them amongst my staff. Mrs. Nance and her son Michael, though, they had the loveliest way about them. Nice manners, nicely dressed, marvelous, attractive people. (Twice, other guests at the hotel mistook her for Diane Sawyer.) Naturally, they were restless; Michael in particular was a fidgety one. He liked to slip into the hotel's pool and stay out there for a half an hour at a time, just swimming laps back and forth until it exhausted him. Then, he might return to their cabana and order a pitcher of martinis. He'd fall asleep on a chaise longue, and our Tiki Lounge bartender, Bobby Ray, said the fishing boats way out at the horizon probably heard the snoring. Michael might get into the water again after he awakened. On one occasion, I saw Mrs. Nance walk along the pool's edge in her royal blue one-piece swimsuit, a light green, gauzy sarong tied around her waist. She carried a towel over to the deep end where Michael was doing laps. When he saw her, he immediately aimed for the ladder. He climbed out, accepted the towel, and began to dry off.

My second year at the Carolinian, they returned again in late May, and this was when we actually had the issue with them. The problem would have been avoided completely if Mrs. Nance had simply hung the DND sign out on her door. Or if our maid on that floor, Kayla Shuler, had followed a company policy, which clearly states,

> Before a maid is to open a door, she is to listen for a moment. If she hears the slightest noise from inside the room, she is to move on to the next room. When she unlocks the door, she is to open it and say Good morning! And then she is to wait another moment for an answer.

Kayla later claimed she followed the rules. She opened the door and said good morning and then eased the maid's cart into the little hallway of the room. She caught something in the mirror hanging on the wall opposite the king-sized bed. Then, in the mirror's reflection, she saw someone sitting up. "My god, get out of here!" Kayla said they both yelled at her. This was what she explained to the day assistant manager, Wayne Samuelson, a kid just out of Wake who was already shooting for my job. Wayne explained Kayla's story to me after he called the main office in Dallas. Then, while Wayne was in my office, I received a call from Dallas myself. On the other end was a company lawyer, a Mr. Hanover. He said, "Look, handle it. Tell the staff to keep quiet. Do you understand? Good lord." After I hung up, I could only stare at Wayne. Young kid, early twenties, always with an answer.

"Why didn't you just tell me?" I said. "Why call Dallas?"

"Couldn't find you," he said. I was about to ask him again and his mouth opened. He said, "I came in on Kayla babbling to a couple of other staff members, getting them worked up. They suggested I call Dallas. Not bother you with it."

"I'm not satisfied with your explanation," I said.

"We didn't think you would do anything about it," he said. "The customer is always right." He smirked after he said that.

I said to him, "Please get out of this office right now." I was stunned by his behavior. Just speechless. My first thought was that he should be fired for insubordination. But since he was management in training, I would have to get approval from Dallas. The kid was a head-to-tail copperhead, but they wouldn't let him go just because of that. I thought, hoped, either Mrs. Nance or Michael would call down to the front desk and say they were checking out immediately. Save everyone. I stayed in my office for half an hour, then phoned the front desk clerk, Helen Dolphin, asked her how things were going. What Kayla had seen was all over the hotel by now and Helen understood what I meant.

"Not a peep," she said.

I said, "The Nances are in 729 and 731, yes?"

She said, "Wow, you memorize every guest like that?"

I said, "No, I don't." After a pause, I decided to hang up. Helen was just a year younger than myself, with intriguing clay-colored skin, shining black hair, a smile that put people at ease. A natural for the front desk. As I rode the elevator to the seventh floor, I supposed I should've asked her which Nance had which room, but I imagined it didn't matter. Sometime, I thought, I will call Helen to my office and tell her not to let this business with the Nances make her feel strange about the kind of place we are running here or the resort life overall. My heart was beating fast when I tapped on 729 first and heard steps and, when the door opened, Mrs. Nance stood there dressed in a khaki skirt and ivory-and-blue-striped silk blouse, her thick blond hair all swept back. Her aqua eyes seemed hectic and exhausted. Faint eyebrows sharpened towards her nose.

Mrs. Nance: Oh, have you seen Michael?

Me: No, I'm sorry. How are you?

Mrs. Nance: I am fine. How are you?

Me: I'm all right. Where is Michael?

Mrs. Nance: I don't keep track of his every moment on this earth. I thought you might be him. He's probably running out on the beach.

Me: It's good to stay in shape.

Mrs. Nance: You're here about the maid barging in. That's all right, I've already forgotten about it. No harm.

Me: She said there was no sign on the door.

Mrs. Nance: My attorney's name is Mr. Levy... Perhaps.... Do you live in this hotel? I've stayed in hotels where the manager has a room to himself. In Europe, it's like that. There to help you all the time. Back in Buffalo, Michael lives all the way across town from me. He has a girlfriend named Shauna.

Me: There are non-hotel lives. I live in an apartment building further inland, about a mile away. At night, I do something quiet, read a book, watch a DVD.... If I'm being honest, I can't say I'm surprised by any of this.

Mrs. Nance: That is a terrible thing to say.

Me: Being honest?

Mrs. Nance: Well, yes. What did you mean?

Me: You could've stopped all this.

Mrs. Nance: You never know something is too much until it's too late.

Me: You know. How would you not know?

Mrs. Nance: You run a hotel. And not a great one, sir.

Me: I'm sending up a bellman.

Mrs. Nance: No. Do you understand? Michael will return and when he does, I will call down to the front desk. Do you understand? We will leave when we are ready.

Me: I would appreciate it if you didn't come back here.

Mrs. Nance: Once we leave, you'll never see us again. How's that? And don't you say a word to Michael. Don't you upset him.

Me: Goodbye.

Mrs. Nance: Get out of here.

I supposed if they left one hour or three hours from now, it wouldn't make any difference. I was just glad no one but her could hear the sound in my voice. I left that room and I walked up the hallway of the seventh floor. The service elevator was the closest one and I stepped inside that, pressed B, started my descent. I had an odd thought about blackmailing the Nances. How easy that might be. They could just send me a check, once a year. I wouldn't have to work another day for the rest of my life. But what would I do? Learn to play an acoustic guitar? Wear cut-off jean shorts and just be a beach guy who liked to sleep out under the stars? The elevator doors opened for the basement and I faced the laundry room.

There were two full carts of linen still to be washed. A couple of the maids, Brandi and Maria, were propped along the edges of the folding table. Maria smoked a cigarette, which was absolutely forbidden inside the building. She dropped the cigarette into the can of soda she held. The two of them were on their sneakered feet, padding for the machines.

I walked up a flight of stairs, then down the long hallway past my own office, made a right, pushed the door open to the outside. I walked past the swimming pool and the cabanas and wound up at the edge of the Tiki Lounge, looking out to the beach and the ocean beyond it. I had a picture in my head of Michael Nance running, just running until he was exhausted, losing track of how far he'd gone.

"You okay there, boss?" a voice said, and I stayed in place. Boss? I thought. One summer, when I was still a teenager, I worked at my father's dry-cleaning business on Woodward Avenue in downtown Detroit. Everyone called him boss, though they did this in a certain way, as if to give him confidence.

"I'm not my father," I said aloud. When I turned, I said, "Please, call me Anthony." The person I said this to was Bobby Ray, the silver-haired bartender of our Tiki Lounge with its bamboo-hut motif. He stood behind the counter, manning the row of bottles lined up in front of a little wall made of plastic palm fronds. After five, Bobby Ray folded it all up like a city corner newsstand. In the evenings, he put on a dark vest and worked inside, in the Meteor. I watched the beach for a time and then turned to look at Bobby Ray again. "You think I'm a good manager?" I said. This question caught us both off guard. But he did what a good bartender does: he smiled in a knowing way.

Still, it took him longer to respond than I would've liked. He finally said, "Best manager in the world is a ghost. People think he isn't around, but he is." He was a bartender; advice was reflex.

70

I said, "You think I don't try for that?"

Bobby Ray said, "You look kinda warm in that jacket, Anthony. Lemme get you a cranberry juice."

I squared my shoulders to the shoreline again. "My hotel feels a little shabby to me today," I said. I felt tired after saying it. I felt as if I hadn't slept in a month. My back was all tingly. I wondered how much better the ocean would make me feel. The water out there seemed dark. There was an endlessness to it. And people usually complained that it was cold. I turned to see if Bobby Ray had heard me. He'd already walked down to the far end of the bar counter. He lifted the ice scoop, filled a tall glass with cubes. He poured in cranberry juice, set a lime wedge on top. To my surprise, he reached for the vodka bottle and poured in two fingers of that. He set the drink on an emerald green cocktail napkin. In a moment, I stepped over to it. I'd never had a drink on the job in my life, not even when I worked in New Orleans. Of course, I drank liquor, knew what a vodka and cranberry tasted like. I just didn't want to get a bad habit started. I lifted the glass, took a sip, then another, and set it down again. "Pretty good," I said. "Thank you." I decided to take another sip. After I sat the glass down again, I said, "Sort of a large knife there, Bobby." He held it up. The blade was as clear as a mirror, and it held a tiny burning ball of sunlight.

"We have an island theme here," he said. "I want it to seem authentic. Know what I mean?"

I said, "I suppose I do. It's your island, right?"

"You'd be surprised how my guests behave," he said.

I supposed he could've meant this one of two ways, but all I said was, "Thanks for the drink." I walked past the bar, then down the wide sandy path between the lines of cabanas. I strolled alongside our swimming pool, which for some reason was unused at the moment. The pool was Guests Only, and we kept the water heated and sparkling. A couple of weeks ago, a cabana boy—I always forgot his name—had asked about having have a pool party out here, just him and a few of his friends who usually worked nights. They would have the party on a weekday. "We'll play our music soft," he said. "Just a little dancing. We want to go swimming."

I stared at his silly, young face. It seemed to equal the truth about any number of things. I pointed and said, "Swimming? See that out there? That's the Atlantic and it's just waiting for you and your friends." He'd been grinning, and as I spoke his expression fell.

There had been a better way to handle it, and I guessed that was the thing with me. The rules of the hotel kept telling me what to say, but they didn't apply all the time, not even the policies of the best resort out there. Anyway, I should've fixed things, not left the cabana boy feeling scolded. I could've offered an idea about the pool—that people worked their way up to getting to swim in it. I thought of the pool now, the clean, shimmering water. I should've nodded in the direction of the Atlantic and said, Look, that ocean, it's waiting for me, too.

Prodigy

Molly left an audio guide, the type rented at a museum, on the dining room table. Upstairs, her closet was empty. Gone were her toiletry articles, everything from the nightstand on her side of the bed. The man had been in Raleigh for four days, giving lectures at a conference. He knew something like this could happen. Molly was twenty-six, an age that everyone said was too young for him. He had tried to keep up with her, wanted her to be fascinated by everything. He took her to many museums. The guide Molly left for him had an orange cord that could be looped over one's neck. The man sat on the couch in his living room. He understood: there had been too much of this. But it was what he knew. He could not think of anything else to do now, so he pulled on the headphones, touched the green button. A genteel, male, Southern voice said, *You are about the enter the home of Elvis Presley. Please stay behind the partitions. Do not step into the rooms. The upstairs is closed to visitors. Once you are inside the house, press 7.* The man decided to press 7. He listened, then pressed 8 to hear about the TV room. He found information on the billiard room on 10; the story behind the "jungle" room on 12.

The man remembered the weekend he and Molly took the trip to Memphis. It was just a few months ago, the quiet month of February. The trip was a lark, just this silly thing to try. Back in their rental car, with the heater going, he said the house struck him as a strange, American-style celebration of loneliness. She immediately agreed. She unzipped her jacket, revealed the audio guide, the headphones snug around her neck. Forgot to turn these back in. Souvenir, she said. Thief, the man said.

He removed the headphones and sat quietly on the couch. He

thought, okay, I understand. I get it. Molly knew him and she knew how to be kind to him. His heart turned. This one is going to hurt, he thought. He attempted to steel himself. But then he allowed his mind to drift. He pictured them living in a mansion. Would they have ended up sitting at opposite ends of a long dining table? Parents? he thought. My parents? Living in the same house with us? My mother and father sharing a bedroom? Together?

His mother preferred solitude. She liked museums, the quiet inside them, he remembered that. She was a good mother. They rode the city bus to as many places as she could find. He thought of the sound of her voice, her hand gesturing to a painting by Léger. Do you understand? she said, in a whisper.

He'd been something of a prodigy. Yes, Mother, he had said. In part, it appears to be a whimsical machine. Her voice, barely audible, replied, Of course. She whispered this too, though she did not have to say the words at all. She wanted some things to speak for her. Even back then, he could sense it.

Confetti

Rachel, Joe, and I rode in my little Toyota for Turfway Park on an icy February afternoon, the three of us in dark topcoats. We chatted in a good-natured way about gambling and the bad weather and the lack of a variety of things to do in general, and then Rachel, from nowhere, leaned forward from the back seat and stuck her head in the space between Joe's left shoulder and my right and said to him, "Kenny here thinks the horse you like might be in trouble today."

Right away, I said, "I just have a few doubts overall." My eyes went to the rear-view where Rachel was smiling and blinking her big hazel eyes at me.

"And one is serious," she said.

Joe Grovey had been sitting with his head bowed. He sat like this a lot of the time. He was blind. He had been blind since he was a small boy; that was the story. He was perhaps sixty years old now. "Do tell," he said.

I exhaled. "She and I were just fooling around last night."

"I would hope so," Joe said.

With a loose fist, Rachel knocked him on the bicep. Rachel was in her mid-thirties. Her bookmaker father, Buster Corbett, had been friends with Joe for decades. Though Buster couldn't be wild about his daughter hanging around with gamblers, he also understood that she knew how to take care of herself. Buster had another commitment today, so he'd asked her to take Joe to the track. Joe had a horse he wanted to bet. He was a bridge-jumper, a man who would occasionally put down a huge wager to make just a little profit. In my opinion, this could be a nerve-racking thing.

"Come on," he said.

Rachel touched my elbow with the back of her hand. I wanted to say something, just not about this particular horse. For as long as anyone could remember, Joe had been playing the races. He had been a masseur at a private athletic club until he retired a year ago. He had strong, enormous hands.

I said, "I was just trying to be a big shot." After a moment, I felt myself shrug. "I always try to beat the favorite, Joe, you know that."

All around us, the Kentucky countryside was still blanketed from last week's snowfall. The snow was always pretty in the way it arrived. The whiteness of everything made me feel a certain way, and it hit me then that I loved both Rachel and Joe, though in crazily different categories. It suddenly felt as if I had the exact right two people in my life right now. If we weren't heading for the racetrack, I might have believed something else. But we were.

Turfway had been closed since the snowstorm. The roads were clear now and the radio said the track surface was in good shape. Everyone seemed restless. Rachel had invited me over last night, and her father had called while I was there. He'd said Joe had picked out a bridge-jumper horse. Rachel offered to answer phones for her father if he wanted to take Joe to the races, I heard her say that. You had to change how you looked at things when you were around Joe, and sometimes people were not in the mood for that. Finally, she said to her father, okay, all right, I'll do it.

When Rachel told me the name of the horse, Blue Brigade, I immediately became interested. The best sprinter on the grounds. Blue Brigade would be racing a one-mile distance this time, so he would be trying to stretch his speed around two turns. I knew plenty about this horse: a tiny, steel-gray colt that had been beating my brains out for months. "I was here for its last race," I said now. "Seven-eighths of a mile, won by daylight." I liked to stand out on the asphalt apron and watch the races. I had the ability to notice details of any horse race, which could be viewed as both a gift and a curse. The curse was that they never let you make a bet once a race had started.

"I know," Joe said.

To me, the horse had looked very tired, had shortened stride noticeably. But this wasn't anything I felt like offering. When you said *I saw something* to a man like Joe, it had a way of sounding superior. It was no big deal, but you needed to be careful about it.

"Book my bet if you want," Joe said. "It makes no difference to me." He held a fold-up, cherry-colored walking stick on his lap. His head was turned partway. He didn't wear sunglasses and his eyes went in different directions.

"No way," I said.

"You'd only be out five hundred," he said.

"Yeah," Rachel said.

"No thanks," I said. I was a salesman, and five hundred dollars was a lot of money to me. Gambling-wise, of late, I'd been in a slump. For example, if I made a profit of five hundred today I would think I was king of the highway. I'd start believing the moon was in the sky because I'd put it there.

In addition to white trousers, Joe wore a white sweatshirt and, under his dark, too-big topcoat, a brownish-gray tweed jacket. Inside one of the jacket pockets, Joe had a stack of cash, ten thousand dollars, probably held together by a single rubber band. We'd stopped by Citizens' Bank half an hour earlier and Joe had gone in by himself. "The bank manager looks after him personally," Rachel said while he was inside. After she said this, I supposed she was picturing it, and then I was as well. There was some speculation as to the overall amount of Joe's wealth. He had worked as a masseur for four decades and lived in a modest brick home on 9th Street in Bellevue. But, according to Buster, Joe had made a small fortune from his tips. He invested his money wisely. He bought percentages of local convenience chains and liquor stores.

Joe's betting strategy was this: Every other month—sometimes it would take longer than that—he would pick out a heavy favorite, and on this horse he would bet ten thousand to show. The race-tracks had a minimum payout of five percent on all bets, so all the heavy favorite had to do was finish first, second, or third. Joe would make his five-hundred-dollar profit and try to make it last as long as he could. House money, that's what everyone played for. When you had that in your pocket, you were bulletproof. You were age-less. The world had once again turned beautiful and manageable. Playing with house money, Joe would call in trifecta and superfecta wagers to Buster. Joe would play all these long-shot combinations and because he was a good handicapper—and, just as important, seemed to have more than his share of luck with the ponies— Buster would send a runner out to the track to lay off Joe's bets. Sometimes Buster would ask Rachel to do this. It annoyed her to be a runner for her father, a man who was afraid of taking a beating from a blind guy. Joe would sit in his own living room and listen to the race results on the radio. He would hit something occasionally, once in a while something huge. He'd cashed a superfecta ticket for almost thirty grand just a few months ago, that's what I'd heard. He invested it in a chili parlor. You'd never run out of money if you bought in to places that people counted on being there—this was Joe's philosophy. After that, I guess he started to look for his next bridge-jumper horse.

Joe was from the mountains in eastern Kentucky, and the talk was that there was a little inbreeding in his family; that was the rea-son for his defective genes, his blindness. The Groveys had moved to the city of Bellevue because Joe would never be able to work in the coal mines, and when he was in his teens, he got a job in the laundry room at an athletic club across the river in Cincinnati. He washed towels and uniforms; apparently all the athletic-club employees wore white so it was easy to handle this type of work. Still in his early twenties, Joe learned how to give rubdowns from the old, mute German there and was eventually promoted to head masseur. His table was in the basement of the club, and he rubbed down rich men all morning. At 1 P.M., Joe walked upstairs to the club's little dining room and was served lunch on the house: the day's special, along with two bottles of Red, White & Blue beer. Then, he would return to the basement to give rubdowns until five. It wasn't difficult to understand why he liked gambling now, nor to understand the jolt he probably got from betting ten grand on a single race. The big bets he liked to make in person, be at the track as the race unfolded. I guessed he wanted to feel everything about it.

Nothing else was said about the horse Joe wanted to bet today, not then at least, and Rachel sat back after another minute passed. I guessed that each of us was thinking about different things. I watched Rachel in the rear-view. She sat with her arms loose at her sides and looked out the window on her left. "What's the biggest bet you ever made, anyway?" I said. By my tone, Rachel knew I was talking to her, and she put her eyes on the back of my head. She hardly seemed surprised. But that was the thing about me. I could talk about gambling forever.

"My ex," she said in a disinterested way.

"What about you?" Joe said, and his voice had a little play to it.

I thought about my answer. I didn't want to say anything serious; gambling talk could also sound pathetic. I tried to think of something else everyone might like. I said, "I ever tell you about the first time I took Joe to the races?" Rachel was looking out the window again and didn't seem upset about anything. "What are you thinking about back there?"

"You should have heard this boy talking last night," she said. "Talking about your horse."

Joe said, "Oh, yeah?"

"He said this race today, it's a classic trap."

"Jesus Christ," I said. My eyes went over in Joe's direction, though he stayed with his profile toward me, kept his head bowed. "I didn't mean anything by it," I said. "I just think the scenario is a little worrisome." My eyes went back to the rear-view. I couldn't figure out Rachel's angle.

She could feel my eyes on her, I supposed. She said, "You should book his bet, Kenny. You weren't drunk last night. You were serious."

"So what?" I said, trying to laugh. "What do I know?" I felt nervous then, felt my heart beating.

Joe said, "Book the bet. You aren't going to hurt my feelings. But you do have to pay me right after the race. None of this 'I'll catch up with you later.'"

The first time I ever took Joe to the racetrack, I was running errands for Buster, something I did to help straighten a debt I had built up with him. It's a long story and one I don't really need to get into, but while Joe and I were together at the races that day, I told him about the debt. He'd offered advice in a fatherly way. He'd said, *Don't bet what you don't have, Kenny. That's when they really make you pay.*

"Well, the first time Joe and I went to the track together...." I thought of something and I leaned in Joe's direction and said, "You tell it."

"Me?" he said in a quiet way. "Oh, that." He reached up and rubbed his face. It was the gesture of a man who'd been daydreaming. He sniffed one time and then he said, "This was a while ago, Rachel." She turned in his direction, even though, of course, he couldn't see this. "Your daddy had Kenny here running some errands, doing some odd jobs for him on weekends, so I called one afternoon and said 'Hell, Buster, let's you and me go to the races.' Buster said, 'No I can't, but I got somebody who'll be glad to take you.' So Kenny wound up taking me to the races. We got a table in the clubhouse, we looked over the finish line. Kenny ran my bets. Nothing too big, though. I just wanted to get out of the house for a while." Joe slowed as he talked for some reason. It was as if he were trying to figure out something for himself. "We had a pretty good time. Kenny described the races for me, he was way better than the track's announcer. How did we do on the day, you remember?"

"I probably lost a little," I said. I couldn't remember everything about it now. Joe had ordered a baked potato for dinner and had taken the potato out of the aluminum foil and eaten it like a hot dog, that was one thing I did recall.

"Then we drove home," he said.

"Here it comes," I said.

"You tell it," he said.

"No," I said. "Please."

"All right." He smoothed his hand over the top part of his head, which was bald. Joe still had salt-and-pepper hair at the sides, and his face, except for the eyes, was chiseled and handsome. He still appeared to be in very good shape. It was not difficult to picture him twisting some flabby banker into a pretzel. Joe had never been married; he couldn't find anyone. Supposedly, there was a woman from an escort service who visited his house every so often. He was very kind to her. He was a masseur, after all.

"It was dark by then," Joe said, "so I gave Kenny directions, take a left here and a right there, and then he finally pulled up to my place. He said, 'Can I walk you to the door?' I laughed at that. I said 'I can manage.' So I got out of the car and walked up the sidewalk to my front door and let myself in. A minute later, I heard a knock and when I opened the door, I heard Kenny's voice. He said,

'Are you okay?' I don't remember what I said then. What did I say?"

"You didn't say anything. I said, 'I didn't see a light go on. I was worried.'"

"That's right," Joe said, and he smiled broadly at this.

"You said, 'I don't use 'em.'"

"That's right." He offered a short, barky laugh. He scratched his neck with his index finger and then pointed at me with his thumb. "This guy," he said. "He forgot I was blind."

"I guess I did," I said. It was true, I had done what I had done because, though I'd understood there was something wrong with Joe, it was as if I had forgotten specifically what it was. Blindness was so hard to imagine. You could close your eyes and pretend. But you'd never know. That was the reason I'd done it. I just could not imagine Joe's life as he had to live it for himself. He certainly seemed to know as much as anyone else. I tried to think of saying something now that might flatter him. "Maybe you should be driving," I said.

He laughed again. "Not the first time I've heard that one."

After I made the bend on Pat Day Drive, the glassed-in stands of the track appeared in the distance and I flipped the turn signal. I pulled into the endless parking lot, which was dotted with old-model, beat-up, rock-salt-blasted Fords and Plymouths and Hondas. Gamblers' cars that were just reflections of gamblers themselves in that appearances were completely secondary. Joe reached into his coat pocket and then held over a handicapped-parking tag, which I silently hung on the rear-view. I caught Rachel's face in the mirror one more time and then turned my eyes back to the lot. We pulled all the way up to the clubhouse entrance, and after that, we exited the car in a deliberate way. Rachel walked between us, her shiny black purse slung over one shoulder of her ankle-length wool coat.

Under this, she wore boots, jeans, and a pretty royal-blue blouse. Joe had unfolded his cane, and there was a ball at the end of it that tapped on the ground in front of him. Joe walked at a steady pace for the turnstiles. The track's announcer was going over the program changes, so it was easy to tell which direction we needed to head. The racetrack management always sent Joe free clubhouse passes, and he took these out of the wallet he kept in his back pocket. Soon, the three of us were riding on the elevator for the third floor. When the doors opened, a stream of people walked back and forth in front of us, but when Joe stepped out, everything seemed to slow down; people turned their heads; I supposed they couldn't help it. I heard someone say Joe's name and Joe waved his free hand, continued to move for the hostess's stand. Rachel and I walked just behind him and received quick glances, even nods. It was an odd way to find yourself the center of attention, but I didn't mind how it felt, and while the tip of his walking stick tapped in front of him, Joe said, "Who's up there?"

I took this to mean at the hostess stand, so I said, "Marcy."

Then he faced forward again and, when still ten feet away, he said, "Marcy!" Right away Marcy smiled at him from behind her stand.

"Joe!" she said as he stopped just a stride from her.

"Three of us today," he said, with a quick, Wonka-like wave of his cane.

"Hey guys," Marcy said to us. She was a small woman, middle-aged, with eyeglasses and neatly permed hair. She lifted some laminated menus from a rack and said, "Follow me." She talked the whole time as we walked behind her, telling us about the lunch and drink specials, and then she said, "Here you go, right at the finish line." Joe always requested this spot when he came to the track, which I guessed was his own way of telling the world that nothing was lost on him. After Marcy wished us luck for the day and moved away, we settled in at our table for four. Joe and I sat across from one another and Rachel sat on the same side as Joe, to his right, which she probably did as a favor to him. Rachel was a nice-looking woman, a bit overweight, with a big mane of pomegranate-colored hair. She wore makeup and favored bright colors and tended to laugh loudly after a drink or two. I imagined she didn't want people to see all there was to her.

We settled in. Rachel and I read the menus and the three of us chatted about the different entrees we'd had here previously, and while this happened I could still feel eyes from other tables on us. We seemed more or less to be the center of something. The stands were all glassed in. The tint on the glass had yellowed, with the result that everything beyond it looked like an old photograph. In the distance were the quiet neighborhoods of the town of Florence. Covington, where Rachel and I lived—though on opposite ends— was a few towns over from here, and Bellevue, where Joe lived, was one town past us.

I realized that I'd failed to purchase a *Racing Form* or even a program and the first race of the day was only fifteen minutes away, so I said, "Excuse me for a second," and Rachel gave me a quick nod as if to say *Get me something, too*. I passed the hostess stand, walking fast for some reason. I felt nervous and happy and I couldn't wait to get back to the table. I supposed this was because Joe was here and Rachel had to behave herself, just a little.

She and I were always close to having something together, and sometimes I felt if she could just act a little differently, I would tell her this. Rachel had called me last night because it was cold and she wanted some company, and I'd hopped in my car and driven across town to see her. Leigh and Olivier we were not, but I liked waking up with her. And then she would turn restless. She usually wanted me gone. This morning, I'd thought that might happen, but instead she had said, "Why don't you hang around and take me and

Joe Grovey to the races?" Right away, I called in sick, told my boss I'd double-time it on the route as soon as I felt all right. I was a good salesman, I worked hard. I knew my manager wouldn't object; the guy spent half the day sitting in bars. We'll look forward to your return, he said with a laugh, and then he hung up.

As for Rachel, when she was twenty, she'd moved away from Kentucky. She'd gone to Atlanta and gotten married, and then she and her husband lived in a Carolina and bought a seaside motel, a decision that drove them headlong for bankruptcy. They fought, he beat her, but she was crazy about the guy and they tried to work things out. Then one afternoon he was caught in a room with a fifteen-year-old girl whose parents were staying at the motel. He went to the county farm for a year and a half and the motel was sold for twenty cents on the dollar. When Rachel moved back to Kentucky, it was supposed to be temporary. She was twenty-eight years old then, and her father set her up with an apartment in Covington. Rachel was Buster's only child and he liked having her around. He wanted to look after her. He was a good bookmaker, and though he drove a decrepit Lincoln Continental around town, everyone knew he was wealthy. There was a difference between a gambler driving an old car and a smart bookmaker driving one.

I guessed that in one sense Rachel would have been insane to turn down her father's offer. She'd never finished college. She drank constantly and nothing really seemed to make her happy. Hers was not going to be a dream life, but she understood now that it could be an easy one. She ran some errands for her father, and once in a while she'd answer phones for him when he wanted to take an afternoon off. She was a bookmaker's daughter; everyone who knew her knew that about her. Sometimes this seemed to please her. Then, it didn't. When she talked about her father, it was either with great respect or as if he were the biggest greaseball on the planet. Once, she and I had been sitting up in bed and she'd

85

started to go on about him. "A bookmaker! Of all goddamn things, my father is a bookmaker. I am a bookmaker's kid. I give up. That's all I am." I suppose if you'd set her down in another world, she would have struggled, and people would have had to struggle to admire her. But here she'd found a place where that didn't matter, and I thought she tried most of the time not to dislike us all for allowing her to live like this.

I returned to our table in the clubhouse with two *Racing Forms* under my arm. I sat down and Rachel looked squarely at me and Joe was faced in my direction. "What?" I said. I tried to grin at them.

"I want you to tell Joe what you told me last night," Rachel said. "Tell him about this horse, Kenny."

"Joe knows about this horse."

After a moment of silence, he said, "Speak."

I stared at Rachel. She touched my left hand as it went for the butter knife. "Tell him," she said.

Joe frowned at me.

"I was here the last time he ran," I said. "I stood out there and watched. I just said to myself, if they ever run him in a race around two turns, I'm going to bet against him. That's all. He's a fast horse, but fast horses do get tired."

"Other horses get tired chasing fast horses, too," Joe said.

"That's right," I said, right away. I glanced at Rachel, gave her a *See?* I didn't like the way she was looking at me at all and I turned to Joe. I wished he could see my face because I thought it might've mattered to him. I thought he would be able to tell how much this kind of talk flustered me, even though I was a top salesman out in the world. Selling was easy. It was an act and everyone knew it was an act, and if you bought my brand it wasn't because you expected your life to change at all. Gambling wasn't that way. Gambling was personal. It reflected an outlook for those of us who didn't know otherwise how to say all that we felt. You didn't argue with others on how they went about it. You'd lose everything then. Joe listened for the race results on the radio; Joe couldn't see. That's what we were talking about right now. I didn't want to apologize to him; that wasn't warranted at all. I said, "I just try to key on little things. Little details. That's all it is. This horse last time, he won by daylight, but he was gassed at the end of the race. His jock seemed ready to hail a taxi. They're probably running him long today to find out something for themselves, you know? No other horse will sprint against him."

"He's just so much better than everything here, Kenny," Rachel said. Her tone was different, full of doubt over everything.

"I know. You asked me."

Joe reached inside his jacket pocket and then dropped a stack of hundred-dollar bills held together by a paper band. It made a sound when it hit the table, that's how much money it was. Joe said, "Take it. Take my bet. You can't afford to lose five hundred bucks?"

Right then, a waitress stopped at our table; her name was Penelope, and when she saw that stack of hundreds on the table, she turned quietly and moved away.

"I can lose five hundred bucks," I said. "Good lord." I wished again that he could see my face. I didn't want this to turn into a big thing, and the only reason it was anything at all was because of Rachel. He wanted to show off for her; I couldn't imagine any of this happening if she weren't here. When Joe and I had gone to the track together that first time, we had talked in a friendly way about the horses in each upcoming race, what we knew about them and so on. For the most part, he didn't bet the horses I did. He had a couple of winners and might have gone home with a profit. I couldn't help staring at the stack of money on the table right now, and if Rachel hadn't been there I certainly would've reached for it, just to see what it felt like. It was not a million dollars; I'd never see anything like that, not in my lifetime. It was a lot of money, though. I did reach over and rub my index finger quickly over the top of the stack as if I had spotted something microscopic there.

Joe said, "Now, you need to make up your mind. I'm giving you a chance right here and right now."

For a moment, I really did think about it. I thought about saying yes and what that would feel like. Sometimes you could tell right away whether you had made a good bet. I thought about losing five hundred dollars to Joe, shoveling over my money, reading his face for how he would've felt exactly at that moment. I would feel stupid for trying to beat him. I knew what I knew about Blue Brigade, but the horses running against him today were a bunch of old grinders. That seemed to be the truth. I glanced at Rachel again—if I'd thought ten grand would have changed a thing I might've done it. But I couldn't tell, not by looking at her. I said, "Will you run away with me if I take it?"

She wasn't expecting that, and it hit her in an odd way. She blinked twice.

Joe said, "You take the money, I'll take the girl."

"Right," I said. The table felt serious now, and this was what I had been trying to avoid most. "No," I said. "I don't think so. I don't feel like risking that much."

"Gotta be ready when the opportunity strikes," Joe said.

For a second, I considered him, maybe as carefully as I ever had. I didn't know what to say. Then I said, "I just don't feel like rooting against you today."

Joe reached forward, tapped the stack. "I want to make the bet. It isn't till the third race, but I want to go ahead and do it right now. Get on with things." He sounded as if he had a little doubt himself, though I wasn't sure it was because of me. But that's what you had to do when a little flash of doubt hit, you had to plunge ahead.

"You want me to do it?" Rachel said. Her hand was on the money now.

"Absolutely," he said.

"All right," she said. Her eyes went to me, and then she stuck the money into her purse, stood from the table, and walked away. Joe and I sat in silence, and I looked at him for a few seconds, then out at the track again. The horses for the first race were being led over from their barns; they walked in a steady line alongside their grooms just inside the outer railing. I imagined Rachel taking off with Joe's ten grand, hitting the door and never looking back. I wondered where she'd go.

"She was testing you," Joe said.

"Perhaps," I said, even though all of this was quite obvious by now. It wasn't a discussion I wanted to have. If I lived in a different manner, Rachel might've seemed like any kind of woman to me, but more than likely she would just be forgettable. I'd learn what there was to know about her and then I would think, Jesus Christ, lady, do something with your life. Stake your own claim. But I didn't feel that way about her at all. When she wanted me to drive over and spend the night with her, I did. She called out when we fucked and that was as good as anything. I always wanted to hang around a little longer than she wanted me to, but when she said it was time to go, I left. I didn't want her to grow tired of me. She never said one word to me about my gambling. If anything, today she had been pushing me to do more of it than ever. She was close to being a dream woman, I supposed. I couldn't tell if she truly had feelings for me. I didn't want to ask, because I didn't want what I had with her to change. I knew there was the potential to feel so much worse than this. "One day," I said, "she's going to get tired of us, Joe. She's gonna leave. She'll never come back."

He didn't say anything for a time, which I was glad for. I'd surprised him, and I guessed neither of us had expected that much. Finally, he said, "How old does she look?"

"I guess she looks her age," I said, though I did have to think about it for a second.

"When she decides she doesn't is when she'll leave," he said. "That's what happens. At least that is my experience with them."

"Here she is," I said in a lower voice, and in another moment Rachel was back at our table, seated next to Joe. She held over a betting ticket, touched it to the back of his right hand, and then he turned his hand, accepted it, stuck it in the pocket of his jacket.

"Whew," Rachel said. Her expression seemed hectic to me, and she was trying hard to smile. I wondered if, while back at the window, she had contemplated what I had imagined: just taking the money and blowing town herself. "Ten thousand bucks," she said. She fanned her face with her fingers like a Southern belle. Then she dropped her hand and tilted her head at me. "What?"

I shook my head.

"You guys talking about me?" she said.

"We were," Joe said.

Rachel said, "I'd hope so," and then we each sort of laughed. Joe didn't say anything more about that, which was a relief. I was pretty sure that something repeated would be something misunderstood.

The next thing Joe said was, "How many minutes until the first race?"

"Just a few," I said.

"Well come on, let's pick something," he said. "Everybody chip in five bucks, we'll bet the same horse." Rachel quickly read off the names of the horses in the first to Joe and he announced he liked the number four, Exterminate. I picked the number seven, Go Vegas, and Rachel wanted number two, Ava Romance. We decided to each go our own way and I ran the bets back to the window and it didn't matter because all three horses finished out of the money. We dropped our losing tickets to the center of the table and Joe collected them, tore them in half with his big hands. We tried to agree on a horse in the second and finally settled on the number two, a first-time starter named Quick Buckaroo, who wound up fourth. We ordered some food from Penelope then and finally it was time for Joe's race, the third.

Joe asked Penelope to bring us drinks, and to be friendly I ordered a bourbon and soda like he did. Rachel wanted a split of champagne. The drinks arrived as the horses were walking on the track in the post parade. Joe said to me, "How does he look?" and when he asked this, my eyes were out there already on Blue Brigade. A small gray colt with a big nostrils and thick dark mane.

"Fire-breather," I said, and then I looked to the tote board; Blue Brigade was number four and the odds were currently 2–5, which meant practically everyone in the place was betting on it. This brought a vague wave of comfort. It made me think something would happen simply because enough people wanted it to. It didn't matter what I thought at all. I sipped my drink, held it in the air, and said, "A toast to Blue Brigade." Joe nodded and reached for his glass a bit clumsily and then toasted with me. When I looked at Rachel, I saw she was already sipping her drink.

I wondered if Joe wanted us to leave him alone now. The starting gate was parked halfway up the homestretch and the horses were standing behind it. I thought of how we all might feel a couple of minutes from now when Blue Brigade came in and how happy I'd feel for Joe, that he'd bet all this money and how he had not been after a king's ransom, but just a modest profit for himself. The horses broke from the starting gate and Blue Brigade streaked right for the front, its hooves kicking back powdery dirt at those chasing from behind. The horse opened a big lead as the field went around the clubhouse turn and the announcer said, "The favorite is in a hurry today!" Joe sat with his shoulders turned; he faced out to the track and the announcer called Blue Brigade a half-dozen lengths in front as the field sped up the backstretch.

Joe said, "How's it doing?"

"Speed of sound," I said.

"Gonna have anything left?" he said.

Blue Brigade led by a huge margin as the field streamed for the final turn. It seemed to be running strongly, but going around those turns could tire out fast, free-running horses because they'd have to slow down just a bit to navigate them and then re-accelerate for the stretch drive. Blue Brigade held the lead going around the bend, but right inside the home stretch, the horse took an uncertain stride. Still, it kept trying. The jockey had the whip out and they were two lengths in front with an eighth of a mile to go. But then some horse, just an old plodder named Sardonic, broke clear from the pack and collared Blue Brigade about a hundred yards from the finish. Once Sardonic took the lead, Blue Brigade gave up. Two more horses rushed past it right near the finish. The track announcer said the second and third positions were too close to call, but I saw the finish clearly and Blue Brigade had wound up fourth. Rachel's face was flushed and she was shaking her head and one of us needed to say it so I said, "Fourth, Joe."

"Fourth?"

"I mean it was close."

"Let's wait for the official post."

"Sure," I said.

None of us knew what to say. Joe tapped his palm on the top of his head and then he crossed his legs and sat in a twisted way for a time. The order of finish, when it was posted, reported three long shots had taken the top three places. Blue Brigade was officially fourth. The payoffs were illuminated on the tote board, and they made my eyes sting for a second. I had been too preoccupied to make a bet for myself. But I would have gone against Blue Brigade. I might've had a fortune. I suddenly felt exhausted. This feeling would be with me for the next day or two. I practically lived my life for races like this one, the race where the heavy favorite was vulnerable. The payoffs were so great, so exaggerated, it was as if money had no value at all; the banks had collapsed and the racetrack cashiers were just throwing bags of it at you.

When I did look Joe's way again, he held the ticket, a simple square of paper, two inches by two inches, in his hand. "Official?" he said.

"Yep," I said.

He brought his other hand to the ticket and held his head as if he were staring at the little square. I felt tense; I worried he might actually turn emotional and I wondered how the sight of that might hit me. He held the ticket over to me. "Any chance the teller punched out the wrong horse?" I reached for the ticket but Rachel's hand caught it.

"You know I'm not going to make a mistake like that, Joe," she said. "Want me to tear it up?"

"Yes," he said, after a pause. "Tear it up, please."

She did this, into tiny pieces, too. She held her hand over the table and let the confetti drop. Her eyebrows went up when she saw I was watching her.

"Snowfall," Joe said.

I felt spooked by this. Rachel put both hands on Joe's right shoulder and leaned close to him and kissed his cheek. "Lemme buy you a drink," she said.

"Okay," he said.

She kissed him again, held her lips on his cheek for a second or two. She drew back and raised her hand to his face, I thought to wipe away the lipstick smudge. He said, "Leave it there." He gave a shallow laugh. "I don't mind."

It did look sad, though, and Rachel must have seen it that way as well because she thumbed away the mark. Then she turned and waved her arm in the air for Penelope. "Me and him are going to double up," Rachel said when Penelope arrived. She pointed to herself, then to Joe.

"What about you?" Penelope said to me.

"He's driving," Rachel said.

We stayed for the entire nine-race card, the three of us, though after the third, we went back to betting tens and twenties, sometimes pooling our money and so on. In the eighth race, our little group had thirty bucks to win on a 7–2 shot and this was how we paid for dinner. Instead of splitting up what was left after that, we decided to give it as a tip to Penelope, who had been good to us all afternoon.

The winter sky had turned from beige to deep gray by the time we walked for the car, and once we were situated in my Toyota again, Joe said, "Remember how to get there?" I said I did. He had taken a big loss today and he'd said *Tear it up, please* right after the race, but that was all you were going to get out of a guy like him. We had been riding for a few minutes, away from the track, when he said, "I shoulda listened to you, Kenny."

I thought about it for a second and then I said, "I don't listen to anybody. Look where it has gotten me."

"Well, that's the point," Joe said, and then reached up and touched his fingers to his face. Perhaps he was drunk, but I wasn't sure and I certainly wasn't going to ask.

"You okay back there?" I said to Rachel after another silence.

"Fine," she said. Rachel had Joe's ten thousand dollars in her purse and everyone in the car knew that. It was surprising that things were as peaceful as they were. Not that she had done anything wrong. If Blue Brigade had finished in the money like it was supposed to, she'd have given Joe his ten grand back, plus the five hundred profit. Or maybe she would have done something else for him. She was a bookmaker's daughter.

In a while, Joe said, "How far are we from Bellevue? Just a few minutes?"

"Right."

"What're y'all doing tonight?" he said.

"I don't—" I said.

"Maybe you can hang around with me for a little while," Joe said. His head seemed turned in the direction of the rear-view. "Let's sit up and talk."

"I'm flattered," Rachel's voice said from the back seat.

"Okay?" he said.

"Not tonight," she said.

"Come on," he said. He moved in his seat, tried to turn to face her. "I'm not going to say anything to your old man about what happened today."

I guessed Rachel might say something smart to this. She had the right to. She hadn't broken any rules that I knew of. The only thing was that she could have been more up front about it. "Maybe some other time, Joe," she said. "I'm kinda beat."

"Kinda beat?" he said, facing me now. In my direction he said, "I'll give you a back rub that will turn the whole of you into butter. You'll never forget it."

"You gonna let him talk to me that way?" she said, her voice shallow.

"He is not talking to you that way. He's joking," I said.

"I am?" Joe said after he returned to his usual sitting position.

It didn't matter. I wasn't going to say a thing to him. In a second, I said, "Nobody likes to be alone on a cold night."

"Well, that's the way it's going to wind up," Rachel said.

I waited for Joe to say something. It seemed too solemn then, and I said, "Can't blame a guy for trying. Right, Rachel?"

"Never," she said, finally.

A short time later, my Toyota pulled to the curb in front of Joe's small brick house in Bellevue, and I watched the silhouette of him as he moved up the sidewalk toward his front door. Rachel stayed in the back seat until he made it inside, and after he had closed the door behind him, she got out of the car, walked to the front, and then got in next to me. It felt, just for a second, like we were in on something together. Like we'd played Joe as a mark. But that wasn't the case.

I knew something about how to watch a race; people knew this about me. I just didn't have enough confidence in myself—if that's what you wanted to call it—to take advantage of an opportunity. Rachel had some confidence in me, or perhaps a better way of saying it was that she had confidence when it came to me. If she didn't have this money in her purse now, the track would have it. I watched Joe's dark house for a moment and then she did, too.

"I could see how you could make a mistake like you did," she said. "It's like the first thing you expect." She watched the house. "I guess for him the lights are on."

"All the time," I said, for some reason.

She turned to me at this, and her face was shadowy. I thought she was going to ask me about what I just said. But she said, "Feel like doing something tonight?"

It felt as if I could hate her a little, for a short while at least. Something was different between us, though I couldn't say for sure what it was. We were closer? I wouldn't say that, I would not go that far. "Yes," I said.

We drove back to her apartment building, where the street-lights couldn't reach the far end of the parking lot, and then we got into the back seat and had sex with just our pants down and there was grunting like we were lifting something, holding it just a few inches above the ground. We pulled our clothes on again and sat up in the back seat. I found myself looking to the front windshield. I tried to imagine what Rachel had been looking at earlier in the day, the backs of Joe's and my heads in the front seat. I pictured the sun against the windshield, but the glare was so strong you couldn't see anything else out there.

She was slouched in her seat. I found myself wanting to think of a question where her answer would remind me of why I was drawn to her. She might have been trying to do the same thing because she said, "Do you think gambling erases the past?"

"Temporarily," I said. "You know that."

"I do," she said. Her voice was quiet. She said, "What would you do if your father was a bookmaker, Kenny? Would you let one good opportunity after the next pass you by?"

"Maybe you should have just said, 'Look, Joe, I'll take your bet. If Kenny is too much of a chickenshit.'"

"I thought about that, actually. I didn't like the way it sounded. When Joe sees me in the future, I don't want him thinking right away that I'm looking for reasons to work him. Or that I owe him. He's blind. He could very easily feel as if the world owes him something."

"How would saying 'I'll take your bet' out loud change that?"

"Mmmm," she said. "There's things you need to say and things you don't. When people understand that about one another, they really have something. But I've learned things like that are rare."

Through the window, Rachel seemed to be watching something about her apartment building. She touched the window and it was cold, so when she took her fingertip away, it left a faint crescent of mist on the glass. "You know which one is mine?" she said.

"Third floor, four windows from the front there."

"That's right," she said.

I said, "One night, when I pulled into this lot, you had the curtains back. I could see you from down here. You were dancing. You were swinging your hips like Beyonce."

"I was not."

I held up my right hand and she pushed lightly at my shoulder.

"You're crazy," she said.

I lowered my hand and then I said, "You know, one might see that and think you were excited about who you were expecting."

"Listen," she said, "Kenny."

"I know," I said. "I'm not saying anything."

In a while, she said, "I really don't feel like any more company tonight. I don't feel like living it up after taking ten grand from Joe Grovey."

"I figured that," I said. "What with the fucking in the car and everything."

"Screw you, Kenny." She leaned down for her purse and banged against the door with her arm, but I had my arms around her in time. She squirmed against me and then she stopped.

"I'm sorry, okay?" I said. "I'm sorry, please."

"Let go of me," she said. "Right now, goddamnit." I did hang on for another second. She pressed one arm against the door and tilted her head down. "Don't mock me," she said. "Don't make fun of how I feel."

"I won't," I said. "I promise." I reached over and touched the back of her hand that held her purse. She gripped the handle of it tightly. I said, "I always want to see you."

She sat completely still. "Let go."

I held both of my hands in the air.

With that, she pushed open the door, then closed it in a measured way, and began to walk to her apartment building. She walked until she reached the glow from a streetlight, and then she passed through that and turned into a silhouette again. Some lights were already on inside the windows of her building, and I decided to just sit there in the back seat and watch for the one in her apartment to come on. When this happened, I could see that the dark curtains were drawn. She was inside her apartment. She did not pull back the curtains.

I thought about the time I had seen her up there, dancing in her window. It was last summer and it was hot. She held her arms above her head and wiggled her hips. I'd supposed that she was singing along with some music. At the time, it almost felt as if I was dreaming of this vision of her. But it had happened, I had seen it.

Army-Navy

For Nick Berryman

In the second-to-last year of his life, my father called me half an hour before kickoff of Army-Navy. He said, "You take one team and I'll take the other." I knew what he meant; there was that one Saturday every fall where it was the only game going.

He said this knowing I had been attending Gamblers Anonymous meetings for six years now. "What's the point spread?" I said.

"You damn well know the spread," he said.

I did. Navy was favored by three touchdowns. "I'll take Army," I said.

"How much?"

"Hundred bucks."

"Big man," he said. "Working man and everything, huh?"

"I guess so."

"Done, loser pays the winner by check. Check goes out Monday morning."

"Done."

"Son, you're a sucker," he said. "I knew you'd take Army. They're terrible. You're such an easy mark; that's always been your problem." He hung up before I had the chance to ask him how he was doing. He lived hundreds of miles from me, in a rest home in Ashland, Kentucky. Last year, he'd had a girlfriend, a fellow resident named Mandy whom he also believed was planning to kill him. She'd passed away one afternoon in the rec room while they were watching CNN. "Nasty business," he'd said. "Oh well, I hardly knew her." Anyway, I imagined that if I beat him he'd claim no memory of the bet and if he beat me he'd tear up my check, then make a little speech about what he didn't need to whoever happened to be sitting nearby. In this way, I couldn't call it a bet. When I went to the GA meeting on Tuesday night, I would not begin by saying, "It's been three days since I last gambled." I'd say what I'd said the week before, which was, "It's been six years since I last gambled."

Even though I knew no money would change hands, I watched the game, rooted for Army, felt good when they went up by a touchdown in the second quarter. I thought, Fuck you, old man, you miser. Always kept everything for yourself. When Navy came back in the third quarter I thought of him saying, Fuck Army and fuck you for never once asking if you shouldn't be living closer to me. Late in the game, it was tied, and there was no way Navy could cover the spread. I knew I'd beaten him, and I started to feel sorry for my old man then. I thought of the last time I'd seen him. His room had smelled like peanut butter. I said, What, you love peanut butter now? He said he had an allergic reaction to the bonding cream the dentist had given him, so he used peanut butter to keep his dentures in place. He tasted it in every breath he took. Later, when he had his nap, he took his teeth out and slept on his side, with his mouth open. He looked to be trapped in an endless, exhausted scream.

Navy kicked a field goal late to win and then the game was over. Afterward, the players from both sides stood together, held hands and prayed.

At the Tuesday meeting, when it was my turn to speak, I said my name. "It's been three days since I last gambled," I said.

Blazer

My mother and I sat in the wicker chairs on the front porch of her and my father's house on Halloween afternoon, one week after my brother had jumped to his death from the Singing Bridge in Covington. Dozens of drivers in afternoon traffic saw him dive off the bridge. He did it during rush hour, which I supposed was his own version of mass communication. He sailed down for the water headfirst, and there was no sign of him afterward. Presently, a pickup truck sped by on the road in front of our house and a garbage bag was tossed from the passenger window. Crazy! someone from the truck yelled. It sped away. The Pettway boys, my mother said. I flunked them both in summer school. Didn't finish their Salinger. My family had moved to this town, Burgundy, Kentucky, when my mother got a job teaching at the high school. This had been more than twenty years ago. My father was too nervous to hold down a job. He helped my mother grade quizzes and essays and so on, I remembered that. He rubbed her feet afterward. They both must've been pretty hard graders, because it seemed like my mother flunked half the kids she taught. Their parents were always calling the house, giving her grief about being too serious. My mother wore one of my brother's Salvation Army suits to the funeral, a move that could have been viewed as serious or not serious at all. It might have seemed like she was pretending to be Annie Hall, or the "Sweet Dreams" version of Annie Lennox. Standing next to her at the graveside that afternoon was my father, who was dressed in a windbreaker and khaki pants. He would not put on the one suit he owned. He explained to us that if he wore his one suit to the funeral of his oldest son, he obviously would never be able to wear it again. As for me, I wore a sporting navy blue blazer. After

I'd gotten the call from my mother about my brother, I'd started dashing around my apartment in Nashville, like if I hurried there was a tail end of something I'd be able to catch. I understood I would need to dress up at some point and my closet was full of company clothes, the lime green shirts and royal blue blazers they liked us to wear. The navy blazer was my own, a Brooks Brothers, something I liked to put on any time I had a first date so I wouldn't feel too unique. Anyway, when it was time to bury my brother, we stood there together at the open grave and probably looked to everyone in our town like we weren't ready for anything at all. To be sure, I certainly hadn't liked the way that bag sounded when it hit the ground, and I supposed the Pettway boys hadn't gone to all this trouble to leave us traditional garbage. As I walked out to the shoulder of the road, I could see an animal's hoof that had broken through the plastic. I pulled open the top of the bag. Other severed legs, a few inches of chopped-off muzzle, everything covered in sticky-looking blood. I felt the presence of my mother. Make it wider so I can see everything, she said. I'm not frightened of a carcass. Are you, son? I guess not, I said. You know the drill, my mother said as she kept her eyes on the contents. Behind the barn. Let's RIP this old buck. I'd been burying animals behind that barn since I was in my teens, and to tell you the truth, once I had the shovel going again, it seemed all right to do something that was remotely routine. I'd buried cats, rabbits, dogs—creatures of our own as well as those we found dead on our property. Though not my brother's mail-order iguana. He was a freshman in high school when he got the iguana, and after it arrived, he had this habit of letting it run loose in the house. Once, my mother fell asleep on the living room couch and awakened to find the iguana parked on her chest, staring her down. It wasn't even a foot long. My mother explained that in her scramble to get away, she stepped on it and the iguana died. She brought my brother a sweet old mutt from the pound in Covington the next day, but the dog was run over a week later. That was the end of the animals for him. When he turned to girls, the results were more or less the same. Even the ones he wasn't all that interested in seemed to break his heart. I did hit some soft bones this time, probably my mother's cat Bill Clinton or my old dog Penguin. I dumped the deer parts on top of them and after tossing the dirt back over the hole, I thought I ought to say something. All I could think of was something from a movie. So I said, in a quiet way, We will seek our vengeance on the Pettways. My father and I drove up later that afternoon to the house my brother had been renting, one that sat on the crest of a sweeping hillside that looked over the Ohio River. The landlord had said he'd give us two weeks to pack up the place, which seemed generous. The house had a patio, and right before he killed himself my brother must've had a blowout. There were cans and bottles in the yard, and his stereo was still set up on the picnic table. The black extension cord snaked its way to the house in the dying grass; inside were small messes, dirty dishes in the sink, rumpled clothes tossed in a corner of the bedroom. My mother had stepped into the house just one time before the funeral, and that was to pick out the suit of his she wanted to wear. She'd slept in the suit for two days straight, but my father and I had not seen it after that. Once she did stop wearing it, we felt like she might be ready to talk again. We asked if she'd like to ride to my brother's house and pick out the things she wanted to keep. My mother gave a look that said if she were holding a kitchen knife right now, the three of us would've made the six o'clock news. Since then, it was just my father and me who made the ride to my brother's. We did this for a few days in a row, and, as things turned out, we were not in a hurry to remove the evidence of a life we had never really understood much of in the first place. We had just the facts now. My brother finished high school, then he worked at bullshit jobs. He read Faulkner at night and wore natty clothes: tweed jackets with torn lapels, cords with holes in the knees. Faulkner dressed this way when he wrote, my brother said. He once told me, This is as close as I will get to being somebody. So, my brother had become the town oddball. He wore bowler hats when he went out drinking, moonwalked on bar counters. He held theme parties where people had to dress up as either a famous criminal or a Broadway character. He would blast his stereo all night into the empty country air. That afternoon, on the drive with my father to my brother's, I looked around at the countryside colored with autumn: maroon, straw, pumpkin. I can't believe how beautiful all this is, I said. I just wish it were spring, my father said. Spring of 1965. You should've seen your mother in a pair of Capri pants then. I said, Jesus Christ. He said, Those Capri pants are the reason you are here today, pallie. My father held up an index finger. We just wanted one. I said, Earlier today, I swore vengeance on the Pettways. Quietly he said, You didn't need to do that. Why did you do that? I said, They tossed dead deer parts onto your front yard. After a second, my father gave a quiet laugh. Then he just drove, eyes sadly fixed on the road ahead of us. What would that involve? he said. I'm not sure you can really kill them, I said. They have generations of inbred chromosomes and so on. Probably need a type of exotic poison, like something from an orange frog with a black stripe down its back. He shrugged, seemed to think about something, and then he said, Your mother see the deer parts? I said, She had me bury them behind the barn. Didn't seem to faze her at all. My father turned and glanced at me for one full second. Then he looked back to the road. He said, She dreams it's 1965, too. After that, we didn't speak for a time. Finally, my father said, Vengeance. All right. I'll agree to that right now. At my brother's house, my father and I drifted away from one another. What happened to me was that I went inside and sat down on the couch in the living room. One wall was lined with crammed-full bookshelves, and another featured homemade drawings. The kid from the *Les Misera-bles* poster, Shoeless Joe Jackson, the Pretenders' first album cover. My brother was always drawing or writing in notebooks, but it was always him copying other people's stuff. Long passages from *Notes from Undergound*, the lyrics from all the songs in the U2 album *Boy*. Never anything of his own; it was just like that part of him wasn't there. I suppose he'd felt that. I froze when the stereo from outside suddenly played something from the soundtrack of *Cats*. The music was turned up loud, but just the fact it was in the air was what made me feel as if I were a nabbed fugitive, frozen, caught right in the middle of a searchlight... *The Jellicle Moon is shining bright... Jellicles come to the Jellicle Ball...* It became a spotlight. It was as if I was the intense source of interest to a great many people. Those people were applauding...a tremendous performance had been realized. This was what it would have felt like...if it had actually happened. I bolted for the window that looked out to the patio. My father stood alone out there, his back to the house, his arms in a conductor pose, as if he were getting the entire valley to hold a particular note. I went back to the couch. In a while, the music stopped. I waited a few minutes longer and then I walked outside and my father was now seated at the picnic table, his hands folded together on the tabletop. Nothing had been cleaned up. I said, Hey there. My father had not shaved or showered since the funeral. The hair my father did have remaining stuck out to the sides and waved in the weak breeze like pony grass. He raised his head to consider me. It's so quiet. Who am I? he said. I supposed my father was simply requesting a variation of a truth he already understood very well. I said, Somebody who is doing all he can. His expression didn't change. He said, I think we will try again tomorrow. At my parents' house, I was a bit surprised to see my mother standing right outside the front door with a huge bowl of candy in her arms. The afternoon had turned to dusk, and as my father and I walked in her direction, she had a strange smile on her face. No trick-or-treaters yet, she said. But there never were; we lived too far out. She bought candy every year, though usually not quite this much. My mother stood directly in front of the door. There was no getting by her. She held out a mini Milky Way to me. She faced my father, said, Put out your hand. He didn't look like he wanted to, but he did it anyway. She placed a tiny candy bar on his palm, and before he could do anything else, she leaned forward and kissed him on his bristly cheek. We stood out on the front porch. Our country road was unusual in that it had a number of streetlights and they'd already flickered on. It was not long after we first moved here that some kid walking down the shoulder of this road late one night had gotten sideswiped by a speeding car. His body wound up many yards away, down in a dried-up creek bed. The theory was he crawled after being hit—whatever part of his mind that was working was telling him to get to a place where he wouldn't be run over again. He was dead for two days before anyone noticed. My brother had actually been the first one to detect something was wrong. He and I were not allowed near the road—that was one of the first rules my mother had about the place—but he kept telling us he smelled something. Finally, my father began to smell it, too. As things turned out, it was one of the Klump kids. There were a bunch of them, all raised by an amphetamine-freak mother and a butt-buddy-of-Jesus stepfather. After the Klump kid was found, we were viewed with some suspicion by the people of Burgundy. But then the hit-and-run driver turned himself in. He told the police he couldn't sleep at night, and, remarkably, this seemed to be enough punishment as the guy just wound up with a suspended sentence. The townspeople left us alone; they simply concluded that being in our proximity would result in bad fortune. My mother wrote county officials, phoned them relentlessly, and simply wouldn't rest until they put up some streetlights. Once the lights were up, my brother would torment me, say he'd seen the ghost of the run-over kid out there. He'd been able to smell the kid's remains and I hadn't, so I did believe him in a way. In general, it seemed as if he was aware of everything I was not. I guessed that really had never changed and now it was never going to. The sky above us continued to darken. My mother held the bowl to her hip. Her face was in shadows. She said, Do you think someone will show? and I reached for the bowl. Even though I just wanted another piece of candy, she twisted away from me. Leave her alone, my father said, his voice quiet. My mother walked to the steps and sat down there, on the top one. She set the bowl on her lap. The sodium lights made a faint humming noise. It was that quiet. The lights were placed approximately fifty yards apart, and they made half-moons the color of sharkskin on the asphalt road. In a while, headlights appeared from the west, some car traveling slowly. It seemed to be in part of an otherwise invisible procession and did not change speeds as it passed by our house. Ted Willis, night shift at the Stop N Go, my father said. Heck of a first baseman in high school. In the direction of my mother, my father said, Remember Ted Willis? The way he said it was like Ted Willis hadn't just driven by, though. It was as if Ted Willis had been gone for a long time now. Yes, she said. I do. Son? I said, Vaguely. We sat there and I did feel very much awake and ready for what came next, even if it was just going to be another slow-moving car. I heard my mother sniff one time and that hit me like a punch in the face. I careened out of my chair, kept my feet, then shot past her and aimed for the road. I heard a voice call after me, but I just sped up once my feet touched the asphalt. I took off up the road, in the opposite direction from where Ted Willis had come from, sprinted under one streetlight and then another. I stayed on the road while going beyond where the streetlights ended and it felt like I was just two eyes, two shoes whisking across the asphalt in all this darkness. All I could make out were the silhouettes of the hills in the distance, specks of light from the houses out there. Back in Nashville, I was a salesman. I was not in great shape at all, so pretty soon I had to stop. In the darkness now, I breathed hard, felt my head pound. I decided to turn and head back for my parents' house, and while I walked back, I thought of how sprinting had felt, that when I passed under one light, then another, I had been aware of both a lot and also not much at all. I thought of my brother, his arms stretched straight, heading straight for the surface of the water. The number of things on your mind then would be very few and I supposed that was his point. And then. I walked under a streetlight, and up on the porch, my father seemed to be on his feet. I waved and he waved back. Things kept coming back to me.

Beautiful

Fred and Vanessa got married when he was in his mid-forties and she was in her mid-thirties. They lived in Midtown, where they owned a condominium and raised a daughter, Noelle. Fred retired from university teaching not long after he reached sixty; Vanessa continued to teach elementary children. Over time, they'd become high-functioning alcoholics.

Noelle, a striking teenager, began to receive interest from modeling agencies when she was still in high school. Her parents weren't surprised. Noelle went away to college, in Miami, and when she came to visit her parents she sounded uninterested in her schoolwork, even her social life. Blasé was a word Fred liked to use.

She flew home for Easter. On Sunday, she stayed at home while Fred and Vanessa went to brunch with some of his old university friends. Later, her parents wanted to take Noelle out to dinner but she didn't feel like getting dressed up. In the morning, she caught her flight back to Miami. That evening, Fred and Vanessa sat at the dining table in their condominium for a dinner of fettuccini and Beaujolais. They agreed that Noelle seemed to be getting more beautiful by the day, but Fred worried that she believed life was always going to be easy, that because she was exceptional-looking she would never have to face hard truths.

But I was beautiful when I was her age, Vanessa said. I didn't have a care in the world.

She favors you, Fred answered.

My point is I learned, Vanessa said. Wouldn't you say I know things?

What you know and what you acknowledge aren't the same, he said. Anyway, she's not going to marry anyone. Not as long as she gets the pick of the lot. When she's here, I think we ought to talk to her more about life.

Life? She won't visit often.

She doesn't visit often now.

Vanessa said, Haven't we already talked about that? Anyway, life is about beauty. Wake up, old man. Why do you keep bringing this up?

Last time we talked about it we didn't get anywhere, he said.

We have to agree on this?

If we don't get her ready for life, what're we doing?

She's ready, believe me, Vanessa said. Sweetheart, can I be honest with you? I don't think you're concerned about this at all. I think you want it to be acknowledged that you're worried. But you're like me, you just keeping thinking to yourself my god, Noelle is so beautiful.

It doesn't matter how she looks, he said.

It is amazing how complete is the delusion that beauty is goodness, Vanessa said. She tilted her head. Tolstoy, I think. But that old Russian wasn't as beautiful as Noelle.

Well, he said. No.

Anyway, that's not exactly what we're talking about is it? You never let any co-ed slide in a class of yours because she was attractive?

Maybe when I was a teaching assistant, he said. After that, never.

Oh bullshit. Vanessa laughed, her teeth showed.

I played it straight, he said.

All right, I acknowledge that you're worried that Noelle thinks she won't have to face any hard truths. You can rest easy.

I wish it were that easy.

It's all right to admit it. Our daughter is beautiful, she's not going to listen to us. She's not going to have to listen to anyone. We should be happy.

I think she's beautiful, no matter what.

That's not the point, she said.

When the hard truths hit she's not going to be ready, he said.

In a while Vanessa said, She should stay longer when she visits. When she's here she never asks about what we're doing, what we're up to.

I'm glad she visits.

You're not going to agree with me on anything tonight, are you? Come on, she said. Let's sit on the balcony. The air will feel good.

It feels like I've agreed to most everything, he said.

I know what you mean, she said. Her voice wasn't unkind.

He said, I always tried, you know. The work didn't help. I barely miss it. But I feel like I should be warning Noelle about so many things. He nodded to Vanessa. Go ahead. I'll be out in a minute. I promise, he said.

She filled her wine glass and then slid back the door that led to the balcony. He knew that what he was saying was important, but Vanessa was settled on her ideas about Noelle's life. Vanessa had been a beautiful woman, though that was a sensitive subject now. She hated it when he tried to tell her she was still beautiful. I know beautiful, Vanessa had said to him the last time they'd discussed it. Don't ruin that for me.

From where he sat at the dining room table, he could see her profile on the balcony. She looked out to Piedmont Avenue and he imagined that she was thinking of Noelle, picturing Noelle. He knew better than to keep talking about it, but he liked the look in Vanessa's eyes when they did. When it came to Noelle, there was simply no reasoning with her.

Terminal

1.

The train that brought Leo to New Orleans arrived at the station two hours late. Raindrops ticked against the windows of the coach car, and he waited for the other passengers to clear before getting to his feet. He tugged at the strap of the canvas messenger bag across his chest, pulled on his windbreaker. Inside the terminal, the lights were bright; people were lined at a door to catch a Greyhound bus for San Antonio. A colorful mural covered the top of the wall beyond them; it seemed historical, people working on farms, then moving on to factories. Passengers from Leo's train were greeted with hugs or fist bumps and he dodged around all that, made his way to the far end, the exit for Loyola Avenue, where his ex-wife Karen Unitas said she'd get him. She was a horse jockey, a wiry woman he'd once been deeply in love with. He pushed through the revolving door, then found himself outside, where he stayed under the roof overhang. His cell said no new messages. Down the street, a line of taxis waited along a curb and a motorcycle darted past them. For a second, its headlight beamed right at Leo, and then the bike halted along the curb, just in front of where he stood. Karen flipped up the visor on her salmon-colored helmet. "It's me!" she said. They hadn't been in one another's presence in eight years, but they were Facebook friends. She had a half-dozen photo albums posted on her page, though the motorcycle hadn't appeared in any of them. He stepped out into the rain and she gave a quick nod to the side box; he opened the lid, saw a baseball cap, a slicker. He adjusted the cap to fit his head and decided the windbreaker he had on was enough. Then he eased on behind her, circled his arms just above her hips.

The streets had low spots, ragged patches, and he held Karen in a loose way as the raindrops tapped at the bill of his cap. They zipped down a wet, spongy-looking street, then passed a huge church with floodlights illuminating its facade. They hit a clot of traffic ready to turn onto Canal, and he watched the drops ping atop her metallic helmet. He thought she might say something about where they were headed. She'd talked him into coming here, and outside of the betting he planned to do he didn't want—and probably wouldn't be offered—a say in much. The traffic light dropped to green; she shot across Canal, took a narrow street, then approached a stop sign; at the cross street, a mule with square blinders pulled a carriage with tourists and their opened umbrellas. "Beautiful World" by Mudcrutch blasted from a T-shirt shop. They darted through a half-dozen blocks in the French Quarter, and she made a left onto a residential street. After a few more blocks she slowed, took a right onto a small gravel lot. She slid in next to a mini pickup, turned off the engine, stepped off the motorcycle. He followed her to the front of the building where a window neon said "Bayou Tavern."

Karen pulled off her helmet when they were inside, kept her profile to him and said, "There's our table." He stayed a step behind, allowed her to sit first. At the table, he pulled off the ballcap, removed his windbreaker and the messenger bag. He placed the bag near the windowsill and set the ballcap atop it. It had a fleur-de-lis emblem, like the Saints helmets. It surprised him; Karen didn't give a knock for football.

Their table looked out onto the rainy street. He moved his index finger like a windshield wiper. "This is?"

"Esplanade," she said. "Straight down to the racetrack. My place is just a couple of blocks away." Their reflections could be seen in the glass, and beyond the glass seemed darker than when they'd been out there. He glanced back at her. Eight years. He'd aged, too; he understood that.

"When's the last time you got on a train?" she said.

"Forever. You didn't sit out in the rain waiting for me, did you?"

"Amtrak has a number to call. I knew you were running behind."

The tables were packed in close to one another, and the only other occupied one had a couple of young women staring at their smartphones. Beyond this, Leo could see a small, empty bandstand and dance floor.

"We can talk," she said. "Don't worry." Karen wore a dark vinyl jacket, a maroon T-shirt. The cushions inside her helmet had left faint impressions on her cheeks. Her face looked thin and her light brown eyes were wonderful. She appeared unworried. "How much did you bring?"

"Over four thousand," he said. "Two-thirds of my savings."

"I have about half that."

A tall young woman appeared at their table. She wore a white apron and had a cast on her right arm. "Wine spritzer," Karen said as she considered the cast.

"Bourbon and Coke," Leo said.

Once the waitress had walked away, Karen said, "I don't know what I want to do yet. How I want to play this. What's it like to see me, I mean, right now, right this second?"

"I'm glad," he said.

"You make me nervous," she said. "No offense." She had her arms crossed on the table and nodded to the bag he'd brought. "What kind of important stuff you got in there?"

Money, he mouthed, then added aloud, "Change of clothes, literature, and a toothbrush." He shrugged. "Everything."

"After the race, you gonna make your getaway on the train?" Karen said. "What century is this?"

"I don't know."

"What would you do if you were me, Leo?"

"Do exactly what you did," he said. "Call someone who knows you."

"That is a diminishing number of people," she said.

The waitress walked over with the drinks riding on the cast. "Run a tab, Karen?" she said as Karen reached for them.

"Yes, thank you." Leo waited for Karen to introduce him. She didn't. The woman in the cast strolled off. Leo took a sip from his glass. He mainly tasted bourbon. Karen said, "You going back on the train?"

"Already got my ticket. Thirty-seven bucks each way. My Chrysler is moody. Speaking of what you can trust and what you can't." He looked out to the rainy street again and felt a sliver of happiness. He was nervous, too. Leo could bet four grand on a race, he had done so in the past. But finding a race worth betting four grand on was something else. As time went on, those were harder to come by. "What's the story with the motorcycle?"

"Houston, a couple of years ago. It's a Kawasaki Eliminator. A girl rider there, Ginger Cooksey, an apprentice, seventeen years old, was winning a lot of races. Made me feel ancient. It already had some miles on it then. A symbol of panic. I'll probably keep it forever."

"Sure."

"You been looking at the race?"

"Yeah. It's workable. I don't think you're capable of doing what you're worried you might do," he said. "If that means anything to you."

"An insult, already?"

118

"That's not how I meant it. You don't want to go along with the fix, I don't blame you. But you're too young to retire, Karen. It's almost spring. You're not even forty."

"Save," she said. She raised her arm for the waitress, then made a circle in the air with her index finger, pointed at Leo. She kept her eyes on the bar. "You can use another one, right? Long rides make it hard to sleep."

All he could think to say was "Thanks."

"I never said I wanted to be a jockey forever. I can't remember saying that once in my entire life."

"You never had to."

She smiled. "That hurts. Coming from you, I mean. You're not turning into a nasty drunk are you, Leo?"

"I drink alone," he said. She tilted her head down as if she were looking at him over reading glasses. "I'm just saying what I know to be true."

"How do I go out?" she said. "On a stretcher? In a hearse? I've been thinking about that. A filly I'm on snaps an ankle, I'm in a body cast for a year."

"That's been true since you started."

"I feel it now. I think about it now."

"Then maybe it is time to get out." He didn't want to act unpleasantly. What she needed from him on this trip were ideas on how to make the most money possible. She'd said that on the phone.

The waitress brought over another drink for him. Karen said, "This is my ex-husband. He lives over in Birmingham. What do you do over there, sweetheart? I forget."

"Manager of pari-mutuel clerks." The waitress frowned. He said, "At sort of a ghost-town greyhound track."

The waitress said, "Dogs? Ghosts?"

"Pretty primitive," he said. "That's what I mean."

119

"Bring us the check in a little while," Karen said. "After he has one more round."

"Of course."

She headed for the bar and Leo said, "I know you're trying to get me drunk now."

Karen said, "There's something I got to tell you. We have to share a bed. I rent a room just down the street, but it's pretty small."

"If you want to be married to me again, just say so, Karen."

Her expression seemed patient. "I don't want you to make a move on me and feel all rejected. I want your confidence high."

"Suppose I want to?"

"I know I look good," she said.

"I'm glad you called. I think we got a line on this, Karen."

"I need this one to work out," she said.

2.

In bed that night, she wore gym shorts and a T-shirt. She liked to sleep with the window open, he remembered that. She set the alarm on her wristwatch, gave his shoulder a squeeze, then turned her back to him and seemed to go to sleep right away. Leo lay on his back and listened to the sound of the falling rain. He wanted to feel like he'd felt when they were first together, if only for a little while. He thought she might have wanted this too, though perhaps she'd already reached an understanding there. She hadn't asked him to travel to New Orleans so that they could light an old fire together, but he would've been all right with it. He wondered about the remaining possibilities for them. He supposed this fixed race was both the long and the short of it.

Two days earlier, Karen had been in line for coffee at the track kitchen of the Fair Grounds racetrack. She was approached by a jockey agent, a man who went by the nickname Thunderbird, and he said he wanted to talk to her, meet with her sometime. He already represented Kenny Melancon, one of the top riders in Louisiana. Thunderbird joked with Karen, said he'd been a jock himself when he was young and ignorant. He said they could meet at a Starbucks on Carrollton Avenue, suggested a time, and she said she'd see him there. Karen thought Thunderbird wanted to make her an offer, take on her book. He'd seen something in her riding of late and knew the talent was there. They met at the Starbucks, took a table for two by a front window, and Thunderbird began to talk about a regular mount of hers, an eight-year-old gelding named Skyring. He complimented Karen on how she rode the horse, and he knew Skyring was entered in an upcoming race. He said it was important to him and his friends that Skyring not get anywhere close to winning this time. He said he'd meet her in the same place the night of that race, and if things went like they needed to, he'd have money for her. Plenty. He said, "I know you want to win. But everybody takes their turn not winning and it's your turn now. My people will handle the betting on the race. We're giving you a good cut." Karen didn't lose her temper, but she reminded him that Skyring had been the only horse she'd won on all meet. He thanked her for her time, stood, and walked out. Karen stayed at the table drinking her green tea.

The next morning, Karen spotted Thunderbird in the track kitchen. When their eyes met, he gave her a nod. She told Leo that if she'd been carrying a pistol, she would have put a bullet in his forehead. That was exactly how she felt. All she did was nod back. She thought about what she should do. Thunderbird had friends; he made important people money. If she crossed him, he wouldn't be the only enemy she had. When she got home from work that evening, she decided to call Leo and explain all that had happened. He hadn't talked to her in a few months at least, and he paid attention to the tone of her voice as much as what she was saying because the story she told wasn't a rare one, not in horse racing. What was different was that Karen said she was sick of the racetrack. It scared her to feel this way. The racetrack was all she knew. She didn't have to say that, not to Leo. "They want to play their games," she said. "I think I want to make a little killing off this race, Leo. I won't feel sick of anything if I can do that. You're the one guy who can help me. Come over tomorrow," she said. "I'm asking you. Let's figure something out. Don't wait to call me back in a little while. Give me an answer right now."

"All right," Leo had said. He felt himself swallow. "Yeah," he'd said.

He could have stayed in Birmingham and, with the info she'd just given him, made some bets at work, split the profits with her. Leo didn't owe her anything. She had been the one who'd more or less pushed him out of their marriage. After he'd hung up, he felt that Karen needed him because he understood things about her that most others never would. He was worried about her but felt pleased, too. Compared to other men, at least in Karen's eyes, he seemed to be holding up in some ways. Leo then called his girlfriend Laura Sanchez and explained the situation without getting into the specifics of the fixed race. He apologized for putting her on the spot. She said it was all right, she understood how things could be. She said, "I was married once, too, Leo."

Karen's room was on the second floor, and when the rain stopped he listened for voices or footsteps, someone just getting in or slipping out. When he'd first come to the racetrack he was a kid himself. For years he loved the life, and when he married Karen he loved her even more than that. They lived in motel rooms, tiny apartments, even half of a crappy duplex. Places you didn't dream of living in yet places you knew you'd never grow sick of because they were close to a racetrack and race horses and that was all you wanted. He felt himself falling asleep and he pushed it away for a minute because it felt comfortable and good to be here now, and things would be different tomorrow because they'd have to talk business, get this race figured out.

When his eyes opened again, Karen had, without turning on a light, gone to a dresser across the room and begun to tug at the drawers. He swallowed while considering the silhouette of her pulling on her riding clothes, and she must have sensed something about what he was doing because she said, in a quiet way, "The kitchen is downstairs. Any container marked with a big K in the cabinets or the fridge you can have. You all right over there? Get any sleep?" She faced him with her hands on her hips.

"Sneaking out on me?" he said.

"That's funny. I'm going to work."

"You coming back?"

"In a little while, 'bout ten. I'll be covered in mud, you can be sure. Thought we could catch a streetcar down to the Quarter." She gestured toward the bureau. "Towels are in the bottom drawer here."

"I think I dreamed you and me were living back in Hot Springs together."

"You mean starving."

She seemed to watch him for a moment longer, then turned for the door, closed it quietly behind her. Outside the room, her footsteps faded away. In a while, he heard more steps in the hallway, other voices saying "Good morning." He closed his eyes and when he awakened again, soft morning sunlight beamed in through the one window in Karen's room. On the dresser was a small boombox, a mini–DVD player. The nightstand held folded newspapers and fashion magazines, and he extracted a newspaper from the stack, a four-day-old *Times Picayune*. He looked at the city news, read a feature piece about a man who'd been a taxi driver in New Orleans for fifty-one years. The driver knew it probably sounded as crazy as hell, but he loved people. He did look as crazy as hell.

Leo brushed his teeth and took a shower, and he supposed the other racetrackers who rented rooms in this house had all gone to work by now. By 9 A.M., he sat in clean clothes on the corner of the made bed in Karen's room. He looked out to Esplanade Avenue where the sun shone against the houses across the street. One house had a front door painted purple; the one next to it had a huge, bright flower bed for a front yard and a yellow LSU Tigers banner hanging from a second-story balcony. He watched cars go up and down the street, and when the wind blew he could hear the tinkling of wind chimes. He wanted to eat something, but he imagined Karen had jockey food downstairs: almonds, grapes, sardines, granola. He took out his cell, sent her a text: *Pls brng saus bis & coff*

124

fr trck kitch! He went to the boombox on the dresser, found a station that played indie rock, turned it down low, then brought out the printouts on Skyring's race, sat back in bed and looked them over.

A little after ten, he heard the motorcycle's engine outside and went to the mirror above the dresser to check his appearance. He lay on the bed again, picked up his literature. Karen arrived to the room in her stocking feet, her head covered by a snugly tied bandanna and her jeans slapped with streaks of dried gray mud. She brought over a small white sack. "Thank god, thank you," Leo said. She sat on the edge of the bed, where he had been sitting a while ago. He opened the sack, took out a to-go coffee and a breakfast sandwich that turned out to be a bacon and cheese biscuit. He took one bite, then another, and waved the biscuit in her direction.

She looked to her thighs. "You're allowed to leave the room, you know," she said.

"I know," he said.

She noticed the printouts at his hip. "You got that nailed down?"

"We gotta handicap it inside out," he said. "Like your horse isn't in the race." He wished he had said this differently. "There's just one other speed horse, Karen. I think they're setting up the race for that horse."

"I do, too."

"So, we start there," he said.

"I'm gonna take a shower. Won't be long. I tossed your clothes from last night into the dryer. I'll bring them back."

"I'm already wearing clean clothes." He held up the one bite of the biscuit he had left. "Thanks."

"Fifteen minutes," she said.

After she left, Leo decided to phone the simulcast parlor where he worked but hung up as the line started to ring. He'd already talked to the general manager. Leo said he might need a few days and right away the manager had said this was fine. ("When was the last time you took a vacation?") At Birmingham, the oval for racing horses had grown over with grass. Some of the rusted rails still stood, but much of it had been used for building a smaller grey-hound track inside the horse oval. The dogs kept the pari-mutuel license alive, and with the license Birmingham could offer betting on televised horse racing across the country. The facility overall was a strange, near-empty place. He knew the gamblers were grateful for it.

The job he had was steady; he oversaw the scheduling for all of the pari-mutuel clerks, was responsible for their training. If he was short a clerk, he might take a shift himself. He made scrawny bets on long shots; he didn't have the money to play like he once dreamed he might. Gambling was always the part about horse racing he was most interested in, and the tiny bets he made at Birmingham helped him feel as if he were still trying, hadn't given up on a life he once wanted for himself. But in his own way he'd also moved on and it hadn't been bad for him to do so.

When Karen opened the door, her hair was wet and she had on clean blue jeans and a turquoise top. She carried a short stack of clothes in one hand, tucked them into a drawer. Leo sat on the bed with his opened messenger bag. He'd been looking at the money he brought. "Okay, just to leave this here?" he said. She reached out her hand and he zipped up the bag, held it up. She took it from him, went to the dresser, opened a middle drawer, and stuffed it at the back of that. She rearranged the folded clothes to cover it. When she turned back to him, she began to rub the towel on her wet hair. Her shirt fit snugly around the shoulders and her hands seemed knobby, and he tried to think of how she looked when they first met because this was how he wanted his expression to appear. She tossed the towel at him, then turned, took a brush from the dresser top and combed her hair over. She used a rubber band to make a ponytail.

"You ready?" she said while looking in the mirror. "What's your girlfriend's name back in Birmingham? Lulu? She know you're staying with your old wife?"

"She knows that I'm seeing you, that only I can save you…"

"Jesus." Karen rubbed cream onto her cheeks and forehead. "You can stop staring. I know I look divine. I can stop traffic. I can stop a train."

"Actually," he said. She turned to face him again, leaned against the dresser, kept rubbing at her cheeks. He said, "The train I rode stopped a lot, without you." He smiled at her. "It kept stopping. In this case, it was to let the freight lines pass."

"You didn't want to rent a car?"

"That takes credit cards. I'm through with those. Anyway, on the train I could study the race."

"Who couldn't see how this was all going to turn out, Leo?" He wished it sounded more like she were joking. He didn't feel like answering. "I still don't understand what happened, why I didn't turn into a great one. I don't like to think about that, you know, the why-everything-didn't-turn-out-great part."

"I don't think about it at all."

"You're a liar. What do we have to look forward to?"

"When you imagine retiring, do you see yourself living here, Karen?"

"That's right. Throw that towel back." She caught it with both hands. "Maybe I'm sick of eating like a bluejay."

"Listen, you don't go through with this race the way they want, New Orleans is the last place you'll want to stay."

She wiped her hands with the towel, then folded it and set it on the dresser. "I'm going to go through with what they want me to do." Her voice turned quiet. "I know I have to do that." She leaned against the dresser again.

"So?"

"Bring your sheets with you."

"You trying to tell me something?"

"I might quit after this. You make me some money, make me enough, I can get settled down here. Maybe try to get a job in the racing office. Be a steward. Take charge of all this mess."

"What are you going to do? Watch other people ride? You're not kidding anybody."

"I wanted to get out of Vicksburg," she said. "I told you that a long time ago."

"I wanted out of Paducah. I live in Birmingham. I make out schedules. I try to stay on course, keep interested. I wish it were easier."

"I'm ready to get outside. No live racing today, only simulcasting. You want to stop by the track on the way? Drop some bets on something?"

"I'm just focused on tomorrow."

"Look at you," she said. "Mr. Discipline."

"Right," he said. "That's me."

3.

They walked together up the sidewalks of Esplanade Avenue. The houses there were large, neatly kept, colorfully turned out. The sidewalks were lined with dark and burly live oak trees, their limbs twenty feet in the air, even higher. Wet leaves covered the street and the slight chill in the air made him think of fall. There were palmetto trees, too, with coarse trunks and minty-looking fronds. The grandstand of the racetrack appeared up ahead, and Leo could see the outside railing of the clubhouse turn. When Katrina hit, this entire neighborhood had been a bayou, and when he watched the news stories he had been especially interested in those that showed footage of the Fair Grounds. He knew they would race again here, no matter how bad things got. They walked for a minute and passed the entrance to the track casino. Tracks could not exist without those now. "It must be nice to live here," he said.

"I like it," she said. "I think that's one of the things that's been eating at me. Look." She pointed to a street sign that said Mystery Street. "This leads to a track entrance," she said. "Esplanade to Mystery. When you leave, you take Mystery to Esplanade."

Up ahead, a bunch of religious crosses stuck up above the branches of the huge live oaks. There were also statues of angels and saints. The statues and crosses were gray or white, the sky beyond them clear and blue. He understood they were approaching a cemetery. A ten-foot-high, wrought-iron fence separated the cemetery grounds from the path of the sidewalk. People milled about in the cemetery, noodling among the long rows of above-ground crypts and snapping photos. *Who will you show those to?* Leo thought. "I wonder if it's good luck or bad luck to have a cemetery so close to a racetrack."

"Good," Karen said. "As long as you're on your feet."

Leo said, "Anybody famous buried there?"

129

"I haven't checked."

He said, "Once, I went to Sweet Auburn in Atlanta, saw where Martin Luther King is buried. It's above ground, in a tomb. Like these people. Only it's on like a little island."

"What were you doing in Atlanta?"

"Job interview. Salesman. Almost had it, too. Down to me and another guy."

"God, Leo."

"I just wanted to try, see how interviewing for something like that felt."

"Please don't tell me you nailed it."

"Wasn't bad. I pretended to be someone else."

"Didn't you and me go to Graceland?" she said. "That was me and somebody. Elvis is buried there next to his parents. I think he has a baby brother next to him. More or less, it's like they're all buried in their own backyard." Up ahead to the left was a Shell station, beyond that a canal. They walked over a small bridge. The canal water looked olive and murky. They waited for a light to change. A bluish-gray marble statue stood in the middle of a traffic island, a giant Confederate general on a powerful-looking, high-stepping horse. At the streetcar stop, Leo and Karen wound up with a backless bench to themselves just a few feet from the streetcar tracks. Light green grass grew between the tracks. Back at the cemetery, the crypts were bright in the late morning sun. The other people waiting for the streetcar carried cameras, maps.

Leo said, "No motorcycle?"

She pushed a strand of hair away from her forehead. "Not feeling like something passed me by right now. Hey, I've been coming to this town ever since I was kid in high school. We took field trips. My mother brought me down here a couple of times. It's torture now though, all these good places to eat, me with this tiny appetite. Speaking of that, I thought we'd go to Mother's today."

"Mother's?"

"Famous," she said. "Locally."

A streetcar turtled in their direction. None of the other people waiting on the benches got to their feet. The outside of the car was metallic, strawberry-colored with yellow trim. It eventually rolled to a stop right in front of Leo and Karen. When the people on it stepped off, she stood slowly and then so did he. He followed her up the metal steps inside the car and stopped where the conductor stood. She paid for them both, had the money out before Leo could get into his own pocket. She took the window on an empty seat for two and he dropped in next to her. The conductor walked to the front end of the streetcar, got it moving. The windows were down and the air felt pleasant. Karen took another glance in the direction of the cemetery. It would be okay for a while not to worry about what was going to happen tomorrow. They were already getting a handle on the race. If Karen ever asked whether he truly thought she should quit riding—and even when he was her husband she hadn't asked him a question like that—he would've said no. He knew they were older. He sat next to her right now. She was a jockey like she'd been when they were married. When they had been married, they'd had the right idea about some things.

"You know I'm biding my time in Birmingham," he said. He hoped that he looked sure of himself.

"You gonna ask that girl to marry you?"

"That's not what I mean."

She poked his ribs with an index finger.

"I'm waiting for the right moment to just...do something." He kept his voice low. Their bench trembled lightly as the streetcar rolled along. Then the cord that ran above their heads tightened and the streetcar slowed. People stood too close to the tracks and

131

the conductor rang a fast, dull-sounding bell. Leo said, "Maybe this is that something."

"It isn't," she said. He studied her face, wished he understood everything. "You're helping me, that's why you're here. This is my problem. My career. Don't get confused."

His first reaction was to say something about their marriage, why it hadn't worked. *Always your career*, he thought. But it was the same thing he didn't think she should quit now. He glanced past her, to a Walgreen's. "You think I'm going to live in Birmingham forever, Karen? I might manage a resort casino in Biloxi before it's over. You don't know." She closed her eyes halfway, smiled. "That's right," he said. He felt like laughing himself then. Instead, he rubbed his hand over his mouth, then nodded. "You seeing anyone?"

"For a while," she said. "I'm tired of men more or less. At the moment."

"I'll ignore that."

"I've only married one other guy, the guy after you. And that lasted six months." The streetcar stopped again, picked up more people. "Come on, let's stand," she said. Waving toward a young woman with two tiny children, Karen said, "Here you go." The woman carried one child, held the other by the hand and mouthed *Thank you* as she slid in. The children looked plump and healthy; the mother couldn't have been more than eighteen. The streetcar turned from Carrollton to Canal, and through the front windshield Leo could see the palm trees that lined both sides of the medians. He and Karen held hand straps and her hip bumped against his thigh. Somebody had brought a box of fried chicken into the streetcar. Leo closed his eyes and thought about the train ride yesterday, how long it had taken to get over here. He thought of the sound of Karen's voice when she'd called him a couple of nights before that.

When he opened his eyes, she was staring up at him. "You want me to run away with you, don't you, Karen?" he said.

She held an index finger to her lips.

"I'll be damned," he said, his voice quiet. She turned her back to him, looked out to Canal Street. The streetcar passed a liquor store, a gift shop, another pharmacy.

She turned, said, "It would only be for a little while. I wouldn't want to run away to Birmingham, though."

"No," he said. "You wouldn't."

People stood around them, others talked; he couldn't tell if anyone was listening. "I'm not in love," she said. He nodded. She whispered, "But you're cautious. You'd look out for me."

His felt his mouth open. Her expression suggested she hadn't wanted to insult him. There was no point to that now. *Maybe you've been around the racetrack too long.* This was what he almost said. "Where would I take you?" he said. "In this daydream?"

She squinted at him. "Irish Bayou," she said. Her expression relaxed. "We'd rent a house on stilts. For a while."

He sniffed. "I'm not cautious, okay?"

"Okay," she said.

"Seriously," he said.

"Okay," she said.

The streetcar route ended at Carondelet and Canal. The air had warmed and the exited passengers stood on a traffic island in the middle of Canal, waited for a walk signal. Leo and Karen headed in the opposite direction of the French Quarter, up Carondelet, then onto Poydras. She stayed a half-step ahead and they didn't speak because it seemed as if they were about to get into something. Mother's occupied the ground floor of a three-story brick building. Ornate, wrought-iron balconies lined the second-story windows. A line of people had already formed on the concrete ramp outside. Before they crossed Tchoupitoulas, Karen stopped. They had a *Walk* and she said, "What do you want to do?"

"I'll stand in a line," he said. "It doesn't bother me."

Her hair was held tight by the rubber band and he thought she looked tired. "Don't make light of my ideas, Leo," she said. "Even if they're not purposeful."

"All right," he said. He glanced to the line again, tried to decide what he actually wanted to do. "You don't have to wait with me," he said. "It's crazy, you're not even going to eat."

"Maybe I'll have a little bowl of gumbo."

"I am not making light, okay?" he said. "I'm glad I got a chance at something here."

"I am, too," she said. Cars buzzed up Tchoupitoulas, heading for Canal. When a clear spot opened in the traffic, she grabbed his hand and they crossed against *Don't Walk.*

4.

While they stood in line on the ramp outside the restaurant, someone passed out a stack of menus. Leo took one, moved the rest along. "I'll treat, but I get a few bites of whatever you choose," she said. "That's the deal." When they were close to the front door, she said, "Remember, when you cash tomorrow, don't do it all right after the race. Their guys might be watching for that."

"I'd just look like a loser who got lucky."

"Don't call attention, that's what I'm saying."

"I know what you're saying," he said. He pointed to the menu.

"I'm hoping you order Jerry's Jambalaya," she said.

"Bingo."

A man sitting on a stool greeted them just inside the entrance. He said, "Don't forget we also cater."

The restaurant's front dining room featured a counter that faced the street, as well as a half-dozen four-person tables. The kitchen area was just beyond a chest-high glass partition. Inside Mother's the line seemed to move faster; at the register, they faced a young black woman in a green Tulane ball cap. Leo ordered; the woman poured him a beer while he filled a glass of water at the dispenser on the counter. The woman gave him the beer, he held the water over to Karen, and they carried their drinks to two empty seats that came open at the counter. They faced windows that looked out to the traffic on Poydras. Past Leo's left were framed photos of celebrities praising the food. "Carole King is so pretty," Karen said. Leo took a drink of beer. "I'd love to play a piano. But look at these hands."

When she held up her hands, he thought about reaching for them. Instead, he said, "Maybe when she was a kid she wanted to be a jockey."

Karen said, "I started the meet with a guy who liked to come here. Not a rider. He ate like a stable pony. I ditched him after the holidays." A woman in an apron stood near them; Karen handed her their ticket. The woman held out two sets of knives and forks, then walked off.

Karen said, "He was like ten years older than me. A total degenerate."

"Do tell," he said. She held her mouth open and he said, "Don't, though. Right now, I feel like finding that jock agent and beating the dog out of him."

"He's probably in the track kitchen. If that would make you feel any better. Go on, I'll wait."

"It would."

They stared in the direction of the photos. Actors, singers, football players.

She said, "What's the 'right moment' exactly? How do you envision that?"

This was the way she had been when they were married; she'd grill him about his big ideas. The truth was that she didn't want to be completely happy; she simply didn't trust feeling that way. "Go all in," he said. "Watch everything, wait for a certain horse. Let it fly. I don't have to explain this to you, do I?"

"Where do you go after you hit it?" she said.

House on stilts, he wanted to say. Enough with that, though. "I just want to hit it," he said.

As he spoke, she looked out to the street. The sunlight played on the side of her face. She said, "I arrived here a couple of days before the meeting began. I found that room to rent, and the stables I wanted to start riding for hadn't shipped in yet. The first morning I woke up in that room, it was still dark, not even five in the morning. It's just when I get up. I decided to get on my Kawasaki and ride down here to the Quarter. Drunks were still milling around, young kids mostly, and I tried not to run over them. I rode up and down the streets and then I decided I wanted to be up on the levee when the sun came up, and I parked my ride and walked up, found a bench. I was excited, I guess a little afraid, too. Just by myself, in the shadows. People slept out on the levee. I could hear voices, too. People laughing. I walked down to Cafe DuMonde, got a coffee, felt a little better and went back to the levee. When the sun came up, the way the light hit it the river water looked like the color of steel. Pretty good. Then, I got on my motorcycle and rode around the streets of the Quarter again. Foggy down there. The street sweepers were going through. I idled at a stop sign to let a sweeper pass and then I heard church bells ringing. Everything was covered by the fog and I heard the bells and I wanted to go in that direction. It seemed like something I shouldn't ride away from. The bells were from St. Louis Cathedral. Seven A.M. mass. I pulled to the curb and watched other people going in the church. I watched for a while. I wondered why I didn't wish for something like that for myself. Be a believer. Think about how different my life would be."

"Those people don't believe, either."

"Jesus, let 'em have that."

A waitress stood near them holding a huge bowl of jambalaya. "This is hot," she said.

"Oh," Karen said. She reached out, took the bowl using both hands. "Give her something," she said. Leo reached for his pocket; a five was the smallest he had.

"Not suppose ta," the woman said, pointing to a sign at the counter that read, "No Tipping." Leo held out the five. She accepted it, left them.

Karen said, "After the races tomorrow, I'd like you to go back to my room and wait for me. I'm gonna go back to the jocks' quar-

137

ters, hang out, see if I can catch another mount. What I always do. Don't call me."

"Man, she's right, that's hot. Good though. What are you gonna do, Karen, just yank the horse at the start?"

She didn't answer; she swallowed and looked to the window. "This is a cheap horse I'm on. Skyring. But it's my favorite horse on the grounds. I usually hit it with a buzzer at the start, just one time, then I let the thing fall to the ground. That's all it needs. I'd love to do that tomorrow. Get a big lead and keep it all the way around." Her eyebrows went up. "I used to say fuck you all the time if you remember right."

He nodded, placed another forkful in his mouth. "It's racing, sweetheart," he said, his voice low to match hers. "Take a little bite."

"I've tried the jambalaya," she said without looking at him. He decided to be quiet and eat. He'd finished half the bowl when she said, "I feel like taking a walk."

"Okay. Can I come?"

"Yeah," she said, though he barely heard it.

"Retire on your own terms. It isn't time. I can tell that."

She had her elbows on the counter. She folded her hands together, brought her forehead forward to touch them. "Keep talking," she said.

Leo shrugged. "You mostly seem like the same old Karen to me." She said something he didn't catch and he said, "What?"

"Okay. Enough. Jesus." She cut her eyes in his direction. "Too much right now. I'm going to take a walk." She slipped down from her stool, faced him, and placed her hand on his knee. "You know where the levee is up there? The river walk?" She gestured to the window.

"I'll call you if I can't find you."

"Right." She stepped past him, went for the exit. Almost immediately, the spot she left was occupied by a teenager in a hockey jersey. Someone in the line said something in his direction and the kid shook his head. Leo moved his jambalaya bowl closer, ate a forkful, then another, decided to check his cell. There weren't any messages from work or from Laura, though he wasn't surprised about either. *Hey, having a good time with the ex?* Laura wasn't a gambler or a racetracker. He was usually grateful for this. Once she had brought lunch for them out to the Birmingham racetrack and then hung around, watched a couple of dog races. Said she'd see him later. She'd been married before, to an alcoholic high school teacher who still lived and worked in Birmingham. She was a kind woman with short black hair, fair skin, purple-blue eyes. "Unlucky in love so far," she liked to say. Once she said to him, "What am I doing wrong?"

"Nothing," Leo had said. He thought it was the right thing to say, but she looked hurt after he said it. Maybe all of this was true as far as she was concerned. He wanted to say any number of things to Laura. But he didn't know her well enough. For the time being she seemed to prefer not having serious discussions.

Leo had gone to Western Kentucky U for a year but Karen had skipped college altogether, and one result from her doing that was that riding horses was what Karen knew best. The difference between the woman he knew then and the one he was with now was that she'd been grateful once. And he imagined this—whether or not she might feel grateful again—was the thing she was worried about. That shouldn't end, not because of one fixed race. The words were right on his tongue now. He wished she were sitting next to him right this second because he would have brought it up and this would've helped her. He finished the contents of the bowl, drained his beer and stood; the kid next to him said something in the direction of the line and pointed to Leo's place.

Out in the early afternoon sunshine, Leo walked up Tchoupitoulas for Canal and made a right there, went in the direction of
the levee. He moved up the long flight of steps and when he
reached the top the first thing his eyes found was the *Natchez*
steamboat, a floating casino, with its ramps down and Dixieland
music blasting from its speakers. The mall and aquarium were to
the right, to the north; in the opposite direction, at the far end of
the walk, stood a dark green warehouse with white letters that read
"Gov. Nicholls Street Wharf." Just past this, the river angled sharp-
ly. On the land across the river were warehouses, power lines, trees,
apartment buildings. Beyond the *Natchez*, a huge cruise ship was
docked. The bridge that ran over the river looked empty of traffic.
The roof of the aquarium was round, blue-green, and faced the sky
at a forty-five-degree angle. Afternoon sunlight whitened one side
of the old Jax Brewery. On the wide levee sidewalk, runners and
tourists went in either direction.

His phone vibrated. Karen. "To your left," her text said. "Just
start walking."

The banks of the river were covered with chunky brown rocks.
The other side of the levee held unmown grass and at the bottom
of the grassy slope were streetcar tracks. Benches looked out to the
river; seagulls sailed around, calling to one another. Karen sat on a
backless bench. Gulls had gathered around her, pecking at potato
chips someone had tossed on the path. She shaded her eyes. "Sit,"
she said. "It's really moving today," she added, nodding. "All that
rain."

Leo looked out to the strong-running river. "Deep," he said.
Gulls moved away as he took a place on the bench.

Karen sat up straight, had her legs crossed at the ankles. She
held her hands in her lap. "Hey," she said, "I'll give you my money
tonight. Tell me about the race." Leo leaned forward, reached for
the folded sheets in his back pocket. She touched his forearm. "I

140

don't need to know all that," Karen said. "Just tell me about the race."

In a low voice, he said, "I figure you'll miss the start. This will allow the four-horse to make a soft lead. In these races, this kind of race, that's what they want to happen. A long shot setting an easy pace."

"Unless its rider is supposed to miss the break, too."

"I left my crystal ball back in Birmingham," he said. "We don't know everything they'll do. But it's not hard to figure out. We've already got a big puzzle piece. We know about these races. The fix can't look obvious. Some things about the race need to be explicable." He spoke in a measured way. "I think they are orchestrating a race where the pace will be soft and the front-runner and the horses sitting right behind him will be able to stay like that all the way around. Remember, Karen, these guys don't want to make a mess of it. They're doing this in broad daylight. That's how you and I are going to play it." He looked around, even turned to see if anyone was on the stretch of grass behind them. He considered her profile. "I looked at the race for a long time. Late closers can't make up ground if there's a slow pace. That's how we're going to play it. If I'm wrong, I'm wrong."

"I don't think you are. I wish I could do more to guarantee things."

"You're doing plenty."

"Yeah, nothing." She tried to smile about it. He felt glad he'd once been married to her; he'd tell her as much one day, when he wasn't just trying to keep her spirits up. Past the warehouse, the bend in the river disappeared into the horizon.

"What are you going to do with that motorcycle?" he said. "I liked riding on that thing last night. That was good, you shooting through the rain."

"I planned the whole thing. Late arrival, darkness, rain. There were a lot of details to it."

"I could learn to ride, that's what I'm saying. You going to take me to the train on that?"

"Sure."

"Where're you going after here?"

"All these questions. I don't know. Maybe I'll go home for a while. Back to Vicksburg. I was thinking about that before, actually. What about the time we went there to tell my family we were married? I don't think they liked you very much."

"We didn't invite them to the wedding. Didn't send them any photos."

"They don't know what they're mad about. They've always been pissed at me for leaving, but that's not really it. It was that I wanted to leave in the first place. We played on the sandbars when I was a kid. The Mississippi is shallower up there."

"After you took me to see your family, we went to Battlefield Park."

"Military Park."

"I liked it, all those monuments."

"We okay on tomorrow?"

"Yep."

"How much can we make?"

"Ten grand apiece is what I'm shooting for. I made out my own odds against the morning line. That morning line is always a tepid prediction; it doesn't mean a damn thing once the money on the race starts to come in. The field behind your horse is very weak and I think this is one of the reasons they approached you. Skyring is 3–1 on the line, but he's likely to go off at 6–5 or 7–5. The four-horse, the one that figures to make the lead, I think the fixers won't hit it hard in the win pools. I am going to watch all the win pools close tomorrow. Every time the odds change, I'll know something.

The four is 10–1 on the line and I think it'll stay close to that at post. I'm thinking of spreading out a few win bets on it, not shake the odds. The fixers are more likely to play the exotics, exactas and trifectas, go for a bigger payoff. The win payoff is what the average bettor keys on. Actually, in a way you're in a great position here, Karen. You're not having a good meet, you need to win as many races as you can. If you're riding a favorite and the favorite misses the break, it's just another example of why you don't win more races."

She said, "Leo, you're trying to piss me off today. I just can't figure out why."

There weren't as many joggers or tourists around for some reason. The river water lapped at the brown rocks along the banks below them. The rocks the water touched turned a reddish color. "I walk on eggshells with the woman I date," he said. "It's kind of a joke."

"That happens."

"I guess it does. I don't want to seem crazy to every woman I know."

"Civilians don't understand. Don't be a jackass to her, though. I'm not kidding."

"I'm not in love with her."

"So what?"

He pictured Laura seated at a table in a restaurant. The last time they'd gone out together, she'd worn a black blouse, a choker of faux pearls. She'd had her hair done. He distinctly recalled feeling that he was not good enough for her. He wanted to tell her as much but decided against it. He felt that she already viewed him as someone who disliked himself; he didn't need to provide further evidence. "This isn't the best life," he said, and when he said this, Karen turned. "Gambling, like I do in Birmingham," he said. "I don't do it like I used to. It eats at me." He looked out to the water again. "When I think about quitting, I just get depressed," he said. "So, I guess I'm mad at you for something. Even if I don't know what it is right now." He held up his hand. "I'm not cautious. I just can't seem to find a way out."

"I needed your help, Leo," she said. "That's why I called you."

"You really think of going back home? I haven't been back to Paducah...in what?"

"After the Fair Grounds closes, I'll probably go to Evangeline Downs. In Lafayette. Maybe Thunderbird will go to Louisiana Downs. But there'll be guys like him at Evangeline. I just don't want to waste my time wishing for things to be something they're not. I hate that shit."

"Maybe that should be our routine. You call me when you get involved in a race like this. I'll be the guy who makes sure you get your fair cut."

"Let's see how this turns out."

"Right."

Seagulls had gathered around the bench again.

"I might go back to Vicksburg in the fall," she said. "Listen, that grass back there looks pretty nice to me. Mind if I lie down for a little while?"

Karen stepped behind the bench, knelt to the grass of the sloping hillside, placed her palms down. There were weeds growing around patches of clover. Leo swiveled around on the bench as she lay on her back, beyond his feet. At Jackson Square, the highest point above the trees and buildings was a cross atop a cathedral spire. Karen plucked at blades of grass for a minute with her free hand, then rolled to one side. He waited until she closed her eyes and then he took the sheets from his back pocket. He bent his legs, held the sheets to his knees, and they rippled with the breeze.

At one point in his gambling life, he'd believed that if he stared long enough at a horse's past performances, he might be able to detect a pattern that everyone else had missed. Gamblers had to be relentless in their pursuit of angles. He'd wanted to find angles but he wanted to gamble—that was the main thing. He studied statistics and speed figures and fractional times of races, and he digested all of this before making any plays. Gamblers could make the numbers work; they had faith in those numbers. They trusted the numbers more than they trusted themselves. A gambler's betting could be significantly influenced by his outlook on things on a particular day, but some players didn't want this to be a variable in their decision making. Leo decided that he simply wasn't built that way. He knew numbers were important; he never ignored them. He just didn't want to gamble if numbers were all that it took.

While he worked at the racetrack, he felt he should rely on anecdotal information. But he could never get in with the right people, the ones who had a hand in how things turned out. He learned what he could, but he still lost plenty. He understood after a certain time that losing was going to play a big part in his life. When he gambled, he wanted to feel something about it, wanted gambling to matter to him in this way. He didn't want his instinct and intuition to curl up inside him like dead leaves. One day there would be a payoff. He never wanted to stop believing that. He knew that in a way such a feeling was a detriment to him, that it kept him from understanding more about his own life. How much did Karen understand about him? Enough, he thought. More than that. When they were married, he'd worked on the backstretch as a groom, hot-walker, stable foreman, assistant trainer. He worked with horses and wanted to be around them because he wanted to better learn how to gamble on them. Karen told him about the horses she worked out, but people on the backstretch knew who she went home to. Trainers wanted to bet their own horses and didn't want the odds to be shortened because of pillow talk between a female jockey and her make-a-fortune husband. Karen began to understand that having Leo for a husband wasn't good for her business. They agreed that for the sake of her career he shouldn't hassle her for information. The agreement was much easier for her to keep; this was his eventual argument. The agreement framed a question: Which was more important, her marriage or her career? They both knew the answer. When to acknowledge it—that was the only thing left to decide. Near the end, they were barely speaking to one another.

Leo's sheets couldn't predict the fix tomorrow; a man could stare at those until the end of time and not know that was coming. Leo had subtracted Skyring from the race and the sheets gave him an idea of what the fixers might be after. The result of the race needed to be logical in some way; fixers always wanted that. But races on the whole were unpredictable. Horses, good ones and bad ones, got left at the break; it happened all the time. This was what was going to happen tomorrow. Just a few people knew about it.

In the clover and weeds, Karen lay on her side. He understood that she wasn't sleeping. After the split, when they'd reached speaking terms, they'd talked more about their plans, what they wanted to do next. She became familiar to him again, though he was not fooled into thinking they were still married. He left the backstretch, moved on to work as a pari-mutuel clerk. He didn't miss the stables at all. He liked being around trays of money; he thought that being around lots of cash all day might even make him want it less. He'd never had a lot of money, neither had Karen. Leo felt certain that after their marriage ended Karen had been part of other fixed races. But for obvious reasons she hadn't spoken about them. This kind of information had been a point of contention while they were married. The fact that she'd called him about this particular fix meant something. She didn't want him back and she wasn't admitting that she'd been wrong to hold information from him while they'd been married. What had changed was that who was right or wrong about an old gripe between them no longer mattered. It seemed to be a particularly unique chance for them both.

"Hey," he said. "Hey there."

"What?" she said, keeping her eyes closed. Her voice didn't sound groggy.

"I can only watch this river for so long."

She opened the eye he could see. "You're not watching the river. What time is it?"

"Two, two-thirty."

She rolled onto her back, looked at the sky and shaded her eyes. Then she reached up, played at grabbing his racing sheets. "Put that shit away," she said.

"They help this time." He decided to tuck them into his back pocket anyway.

"I guess so." She sat up, let her arms fall around her bent knees. "I feel like having one strong drink at the Kerry on Iberville. Then we catch the streetcar and head back, Leo. I have my dinner in the kitchen of the rooming house. I'll make mice food for two. You get enough lunch?"

"Hell yes."

"You feel like having a strong drink with me?"

"I do."

He stood, thought she might reach out her hand for him to pull her up. He set his hands on his hips and waited.

"I'm going to have a gin martini," she said. "With an onion."

"I think I'll have the same," he said. She got up on her own, started to walk down the grassy slope. She waited near the streetcar tracks and they crossed those together. The streetcar they needed to catch was over on Canal, and they made a left on Decatur Street and went in that direction. They stopped at a number of storefront windows, lingered the longest in front of the Peaches Records because they could hear something from the Allman Brothers playing inside the store. When they'd first moved in together, Karen had a milk crate of dog-eared records, hand-me-downs from her uncles and her brothers. Allmans everywhere. She tugged once at his sleeve and they moved on. They made it to the Kerry; inside, the bartender had the TV tuned to a soccer match. Leo ordered their drinks and the bartender, a young guy with a goatee, put them together quick, then went to the jukebox. An empty stage stood at one end of the room and the chairs at the tables faced in that direction. The jukebox played something by Arcade Fire. Leo's drink tasted so good he wanted to pound his fist on the bar and say *Hallelujah*. Karen took a sip from her glass, set her elbows on the counter and looked at the bottles at the back of the bar.

She was slowing it down, paying attention to everything; she could do this because he was here and he could watch over her for a little while. Leo thought of Laura back in Birmingham, of the two of them lying in bed together after one of their quiet lovemaking sessions. If something happened there, if Laura left him or found someone else, it would make a difference to him. He was not in love with her and wasn't worried about being in love with her. Because there was more to it than that. Though Laura didn't want to change him, she liked it when he seemed hopeful around her. Usually this was when he was contemplating a bet of some sort. She didn't need to know about that, though in a general way she probably already did. Otherwise, his gambling meant nothing to Laura. He looked at the line of bottles behind the bar and imagined himself and Laura walking up church steps together on a Sunday morning, each of them with silver hair. During the church service, he would daydream about the races he wanted to play. He could not think of anything else to say so he said, "I still want to win, Karen." The bartender kept writing on something attached to a clipboard.

"I do, too," she said. "Man, I'd like to stick it to these guys tomorrow. Flip everything over."

"You'd always be looking over your shoulder," he said. By this time, they had turned to one another. "Evangeline Downs, huh?"

Her expression seemed hazy and she reached for his forearm. "Good old Leo," she said. "After tomorrow, I'll call the racing secretary at Evangeline. See who's planning to ride there. They have slot machines, better purses. I want to be in a riding mood when I do all of that."

"We get the Evangeline signal at Birmingham."

"I'll wave to you from the post parade. I'm ready to go back to the room. You gonna pay this guy?" she said. In the direction of the bartender she said, "How much?"

"Ten bucks."

Karen stood and pointed at Leo with her thumb. "He's got all the money. Gambler."

"Yeah?" the bartender said.

"We're taking it easy today, though," Leo said, then held out a twenty. He waited for change. Karen walked out into the mid-afternoon sunlight.

"Streetcar's that way," she said when he got to her side. She walked ahead, stuck her hands in her pockets. They made it to the streetcar stop on Carondelet Street and sat on a bench protected by filmy-looking fiberglass sides. Others arrived, waited for the street-car. Leo stared to the left, in the direction of Harrah's.

"I have to piss," he said, his voice quiet. "When's the streetcar coming?"

"I don't know," she said. "Go on, you'll make it. I'm gonna sit right here."

He thought of how slowly the streetcar traveled and decided to head for the casino. He walked fast, went against the light and trotted across the street. He moved up the steps of the casino, then slowed at the entrance and, for some reason, brushed at his hair with his hand. Inside, a woman in a canary-colored blazer sat behind a podium and said "Good luck" as he walked by. He heard the bells pinging from the slot machines; then he found a men's room. He took a leak, washed his hands, checked his appearance. On the way out of the casino, he stood in front of a $5 slot machine, thought about sliding in a $20 bill, giving a few pulls. He'd always focused on playing horses; they provided enough gambling for any lifetime. Had he chosen the wrong thing, though? He'd watched those greyhound races at Birmingham, but there just wasn't enough human element there. He stood in front of the $5 slot, which had a *Laura Croft, Tomb Raider* theme. He felt light-headed, transfixed by something. Had he picked the right things for his life? He had. He felt he had. Good things were going to catch up to him. He knew he needed to go. He walked more slowly on the way out, and once he stood outside, he saw a streetcar moving away from the Carondelet Street stop. He spotted the empty bench where he and Karen had been sitting. He moved down the steps and began to jog in the direction of the streetcar moving up Canal. He made it to the median and ran up the tracks after the streetcar. He thought he saw Karen's face in the window, and she motioned her hand for him to keep coming. He knew the streetcar made stops, he'd catch it. But he was a little drunk and it felt good to run like this was something he couldn't let get away.

5.

Karen had saved a place on the streetcar. It rolled along and once she was finished laughing at him, making fun, she leaned her head on his shoulder, closed her eyes. They passed from the Quarter into a residential section. Outside a tavern named The Holy Ground, a young woman in a short skirt and a red cowboy hat checked her smartphone. Further down the block, on a fifteen-foot-high pedestal stood a statue of Jefferson Davis, his arm out like he was waving down a taxi. Beyond that, children played in a small park. Mardi Gras beads hung from the branches of live oak trees. The beads were gold and purple and green and he wanted to jiggle Karen, point them out. The conductor periodically rang the fast, dull-sounding bell. People waiting for the streetcar seemed to be standing too close to the tracks. As they approached the City Park stop, he leaned into her, said, "Hey."

She said in a groggy way, "Man, that was funny watching you run."

"How you feel?" he said.

"A little hung over, actually. Ready to eat."

"I'm still full from lunch."

"Good."

They walked across the small bridge and then past the cemetery where the falling afternoon light gave a tint of blue to the crypts. At the house, they split a tin of sardines, a saucer of almonds in the kitchen. The couple who ran the house, Sid and Annie, stepped in through the back door; they each had gray hair and appeared fit and energetic. Karen said, "This is Leo. I told you he might be passing through. Where're you guys headed?"

"Out to the living room and watch the news," Annie said. "Come on."

"Maybe in a little while," Karen said.

151

"I'm glad Karen is staying in a nice house like this," Leo said.

"She's welcome here any time," Annie said. "Well, see you."

Karen had water with her food, three glasses all told. Leo spotted a six-pack of beer in the fridge but he knew it wasn't hers. When they returned to the room, she went to the dresser drawer, brought her own money over to him. Nineteen hundred and change. For a time after this, she sat up in bed, looked at magazines, and he sat up alongside her, worked on numbers on a pad he'd taken from his messenger bag. The boombox was tuned to a college station. "I like this song," she said at one point, and they looked at one another right after she said it.

"That guy downstairs looks like a long-distance runner."

"He teaches at UNO, actually. They both do. I told them you might be staying with me for a day or two. You were down on your luck. That I was your angel and so on."

"Great," he said.

"Bet a grand to win for me on that horse that's gonna get an easy lead," she said with a nod to his pad. "Spread out the rest on other stuff, those exotics you're putting together." Classic Karen: *Thank you for your trouble, Leo. I already know what I want to do.*

You didn't need me for this, he could've said now, but he stayed quiet. He didn't want it to be true. A grand to win on the horse most likely to win the race was a smart play. He ought to do the same. On the pad, Leo had been working on exactas, trifectas, superfectas, pick-3s and those plays were good, and sensible enough.

"Okay, all right," he said. He continued making marks with the pen; he didn't want her to think she'd insulted him.

"You'll bet to win, too."

"Some."

"How're you going to handle all the money and the tickets? You going to use that bag you brought? That might stick out a little bit."

"My windbreaker is all I need."

"You're going to carry what, six thousand bucks in that thing?"

"Three pockets, one on the inside. Each has a zipper. That's a gambler's jacket. I bought it in Irondale at a JC Penney that was going out of business. Everything is organized, don't you worry about it."

She said, "I hope you make a ton tomorrow. In a way, I guess I want that more than anything."

"I don't need to," he said. "I hope I don't look that way." She didn't say anything else. It wasn't worth a debate. He thought her expression had turned a bit sad overall. "I'm a grown man. You can give me something here, that's fine. But that's not why you called me. That's why I came."

"You mean to say if I was in deep trouble, you'd ignore it?"

"You're not in deep trouble here. You and I both know that. You just got a little rattled, that's all. We're gonna show them that we know how to play, too."

The radio played John Doe's "Garden State." Karen finally said, "Yeah, well, I don't like being rattled. Not good for me, not good for my business. My job tomorrow isn't that difficult at all. I guess I just panicked. First I got the motorcycle, now I get you. We had some fun, didn't we, Leo?"

"Yeah," he said. "I remember that. We laughed."

"You really doing okay over there?"

"It's a racetrack without any horses. Weird," he said. "I can watch a race on TV and still get something out of it. I still pay attention."

"I wouldn't miss the horses and all that. Not to start," she said. "But I'd miss riding. I'm going to ask you something and I want you to give me an honest answer, okay? If you want, I mean.

153

You got all those TVs at your place. When you know I'm in a race at Sam Houston or Lone Star or wherever, do you pay attention?"

"Not all the time," he said, right away. "I don't check the entries looking for your name, not every day. But sometimes I do."

"You still probably follow my career more closely than anyone in the whole world."

Leo felt himself frown at this. What she said was likely true, but it was unlike Karen to feel sorry for herself. He said, "I was married to you once, you know. Besides, what do you care?"

"I don't."

"When I see you ride in races, you always give your best," he said. "You ride all the way to the finish. As a player, I like to see that. I've hit a couple of tris because you got third money over some guy who didn't see fit to ride all the way out."

She held out her hand. "Cut," she said.

He slapped her palm. "There," he said. "Thanks."

She curled her hand into a fist, popped him on the shoulder, then turned back to her magazine. It was a *Fitness*, with a sleek-looking Shakira on the cover. The caption: "Look at Her! She Had a Baby a Month Ago!" Leo directed his attention to the pad. He guessed he had worked out most everything by now. The numbers could help him feel drowsy.

That night, Karen slept with her back to him. Like before, she wore gym shorts and a T-shirt, and for a time he lay on his back with one hand behind his head. She missed the way she used to look at things and she knew he did, too, no matter how comfortably his life was working out in Birmingham. On the walk from the streetcar back to this house, neither of them had said much, though it wasn't as if they were angry with one another. The air had turned cooler as evening approached. He felt uncertain about how things were going to go. He lay in bed with her now and understood that he would be by himself for most of tomorrow. Today had been good and he wished he had a bourbon and Coke or another gin martini in him. He fell asleep anyway.

He heard the alarm on her watch. Karen shut it off, extracted herself from the bed. In silhouette she eased open a dresser drawer.

"Hey," he said. "What time is it?"

"Time for me to go."

"Gonna take all of our money and not come back?"

She turned. "Crossed my mind," she said. "Maybe if you acted like a tool yesterday. No, I'm not going to rob you, Leo. Not this go-round. I'm gonna take a shower, change clothes, get to the stables..."

"Get any sleep?"

Her clothes were tucked under one arm. "Some. Enough. I don't know why I've gotten so worked up over this."

He said, "Would've been a pretty good scam, you calling me to come over to bring betting money, then robbing me."

"Well, I would've let you make love to me first," she said. "You wouldn't have felt cheated that way, not for a while. Look, I just wanted to have more winners this winter, that's all this is. I'll see you back here tonight. Don't screw up."

"I was about to say the same thing to you."

"Later," she said. Karen moved for the door, opened it and closed it quietly behind her. Leo knew he wouldn't fall back to sleep. Could Karen have scammed him? You couldn't work at the racetrack for as long as she had without learning something about playing people. It would've been a terrific con, her telling him the play of a lifetime was in the offing, bring as much money as he could carry and so on. Somehow, despite the fact that he knew plenty about the racetrack, he would've made for an easy target this time. In a while, he heard the revving of the motorcycle engine, and only then did he get up from bed, switch on the light at the nightstand, and walk to the dresser. He knew she hadn't ripped him off. All the money was there; he touched at it but didn't take it from the bag.

He took the pants Karen had washed for him from a drawer, then the clean pair of socks. He plucked a $20 bill from the money he'd brought, grabbed the key from the dresser top, pulled on his windbreaker, closed the door behind him, and walked down the stairs. Once he was out in the cool morning air, he aimed for the track. He wasn't concerned about seeing Karen, though it struck him that she might be in the track kitchen, in line herself, when he stepped in. He pictured finding Thunderbird, knocking him cold right in front of her. *That's my wife you're talking about.* He wanted coffee, something to eat.

It was quiet enough for Leo to hear his own footsteps, and then in the distance he could hear hoofbeats. Horses churning through their morning workouts. The sky looked inky blue and there was just enough moonlight for him to see the Mystery Street sign. He decided to make the turn. He walked onto the parking lot, could see the white outer rail of the racetrack in the distance. Just beyond that, horses and their riders traveled down the homestretch. When they had been married, he'd lie in bed with Karen and ask her to describe what it was like to ride in a race. He liked when she did this and always asked for it while they were in the dark because he could imagine things clearly. *It happens fast, all of it, from break to finish. When the starting gates open, I feel like screaming. I'm that happy, that scared. In a few seconds, I lay my hands on a horse's neck, tighten the reins. Try to save something. In a race, I feel all the parts of the horse moving under me and I feel very light because there's so much to the horse underneath me. Every stride is so elaborate and incredible. A lot of the times the pack gets ahead. That's not a good feeling. I ride it out, hold myself together. When I win, when I hit the wire in front of everyone else, I barely feel a thing. That's how happy I am. Nothing feels like trouble. Nothing hurts.*

Their lives were in front of them then, and when she talked like that it made them both feel better. Leo arrived at the chin-high chain-link fence that ran along the edge of the lot. Beyond it was the outer rail. He had his hands in the pockets of his windbreaker. Nothing had changed, he thought. He didn't have to ask if riding in a race still felt like that to Karen. She'd have already retired. She liked riding in the mornings, too, working horses out, trying to drum up more business for herself. But more than anything she liked the pressure of a race, and when she rode in a race she always thought she could win.

The sky lightened as he stood by the fence watching the horses and their riders move by him. Daybreak was close; he didn't need to check his watch. Beyond the far turn, he could see the shapes of light poles and trees, and sticking above everything was a dome with a cross on top of it. The riders could see the dome and the cross as their horses came out of the clubhouse turn, and he wondered if they were comforted by it.

No one who worked on the backstretch had an easy life. The workers traveled with the horses; they lived in track dormitories where alcoholism and drug abuse were rampant. At the track, Leo had worked his way up to stable foreman and it seemed a realistic possibility he would become a trainer one day. He would need a ton of start-up cash for that and would have to become a salesman of sorts to attract owners. He'd have to do what he needed to do to win races because that's what many trainers did. It took Leo those years on the backstretch to understand that what he really wanted to do was simply play the races. He supposed this was true for more than a few people who worked there. The racetrack, in the end, hadn't helped him with his gambling. When he left, he knew that he needed to manage his betting in a more careful way. If he could do that, he could have another life, too. Something with shorter hours and maybe not all the mind games. It didn't seem wholly unpredictable that he would wind up working at a place like Birmingham Race Course, where there were no horses or any backstretch workers around. The stable area had been partially converted into dog kennels, but you needed a security pass to get back there. Leo shared an office with the concessions manager and the head of security, and he would look out the floor-to-ceiling window there on occasion and watch the greyhounds in training races. He didn't play the dogs himself; the spidery greyhounds seemed terrified. He couldn't handicap that.

Birmingham Race Course had been built for bigger crowds. The track had first opened for live horse racing in 1991. The grandstand and clubhouse were larger than what the Fair Grounds had now. The Birmingham track was built too far out from the city limits, and as things turned out all the surveys and research about the thousands of people who'd show for live racing were wrong. Few people came to play the horses there, and live racing ended. It wasn't the only racetrack that hit a stretch of bad luck. The old wooden grandstand at the Fair Grounds burned to the ground in 1995. That grandstand could hold twenty thousand fans, easy. When it was rebuilt, the new grandstand was much smaller, big enough for five thousand on a great day. One lesson learned from Birmingham, anyway.

And then, Katrina. Leo had followed the news intently because he wanted to see the footage from the Fair Grounds neighborhood. It was the oldest track in America; Leo had been reminded of this a couple of times from the news reports. They were fortunate to have live horse racing in New Orleans now. But Leo supposed the Birmingham track was something of a survivor as well. There hadn't been any natural disasters involved. Just pie in the sky. But they still turned the lights on inside and gamblers could follow all they needed to on the TVs.

After the sun broke at the horizon, Karen zipped by on a small, hard-running horse with a coat the color of motor oil. She wore a helmet with a turquoise cover and a down vest, and he wondered if she'd spotted him, too. He checked his watch; it was just past seven, so Laura would be up by now, having coffee, looking at the *Birmingham News* online. She worked downtown as an auditor for the city. The train station was just a few blocks from the building where she worked, but she hadn't walked down to see him off, nor did he expect her to be there at the station waiting when he returned. He thought about hearing her voice now. He wanted his heart to leap at the sound of it. She answered on the third ring and he said, "Surprise."

"Leo."

"I'm calling you from the parking lot at the racetrack here in New Orleans," he said. "I'm watching horses work out."

"Okay. You okay?"

"I didn't wake you, did I?"

"No."

"It looks like the problem is manageable. Karen and I are still at each other. But there's a way out of the thing."

"Good, Leo."

He wanted to get into more, but it was so early in the morning. "I was thinking about you," he said. "What're you gonna do today?"

"Well, go to work," she said.

"I'm coming back tomorrow. The train ride over here was pretty long. You think you might feel like doing something tomorrow night?"

"Maybe not tomorrow night."

"But soon though?"

"Maybe."

He wished she wouldn't have an attitude about this. Her former husband lived in Birmingham, and she ran into him every so often. Leo had seen a framed photo of the guy once. She had needed something from a dresser drawer, asked Leo to fetch it, and this was how he'd come across the photo. The man was tall and slender, wore glasses and had curly hair. He had his arm around Laura's shoulder. They looked to be in their twenties. Leo had heard footsteps and showed the photo to Laura when she arrived at his side. She took the photo, placed it back in the drawer. "I asked you to get my silver bracelet for me," she said. She closed the drawer, slid on the bracelet. She gave him a kind smile. "Look how young I was," she said.

Right now, Leo wanted to say, *I wish I was in love with you, Laura*. But that might sound as if he were blaming something on her. "I had to come over here, you know that," he said.

"Have I said a single word to you?" she said.

"It all hurts a little," he said. She didn't say anything, which was all right. "I hope you have a good day," he said.

"You, too."

"Okay. Bye, Laura."

"Bye."

6.

With the dawn came a cloudless, pale-looking sky, and while he'd talked with Laura, Leo had moved away from the rail, put his back to the working horses. He turned again now, watched more horses pass. The rhythm of their hoofbeats on the dirt surface made him think of the train he'd ridden over here. He'd be going back on that train tomorrow morning. As far as he and Laura were concerned, he didn't need to say everything that was on his mind but what he did say needed to be truthful. *It matters to me that you are there. I don't mind the photo of your ex at all. You look great in royal blue.* Maybe that would add up to something.

Leo was ready for a coffee and he walked out to Esplanade, spotted a corner bodega down the street with a beer sign illuminated in its window. He would forgo the track kitchen on this trip. Who was he kidding? He wasn't going to cold-cock any jock agent. He and Karen would have their revenge at the windows. He stopped by the bodega, picked up a to-go coffee and a sleeve of mini-donuts, then went to where Karen lived, let himself in, made it to her room where he kicked off his shoes and got on the bed. He had the coffee at one hip, his notebook and sheets at the other. He let tiredness overtake him. He knew that he wouldn't fall asleep and if he did it wouldn't be for long, and when his eyes popped open again he reached for the coffee cup at his hip, felt relief it hadn't tipped and soaked his backside.

He propped himself up in bed, looked through the pages of his notebook, sipped his coffee, ate the donuts. Skyring was in the first race today and the race would be at six furlongs. It would take a little over one minute to complete. He'd made extensive notes on each starter in the race—except Skyring. He had practically memorized past performance lines for these horses. There was nothing left to study and he knew it. There was the nervousness that always came with making a significant wager. When he was coming up in the world, Leo couldn't wait for the races to start on a day like this. He sat up in bed now and understood that the races would start soon enough. His life might not get any better. He was going to make a big bet today and he would be playing with an edge. He was about to do something good for a woman he'd once promised he'd stay with forever. When he got back to Birmingham, he and Laura might be able to keep going; nothing was settled there. It was all right to think about things like this because in a while it would be time to leave for the track, and when he did, he needed to have all of this out of his system. He needed to be cool and focused and take care of details. He had all the bets figured out, but there were other decisions he needed to make. He didn't want to send through all of his win money on the four-horse at one time; those bets should be spread out so they wouldn't rattle the odds. When it was time to collect, that needed to be done a certain way, too. Karen was spot-on there. He didn't need to call attention to himself.

He thought of the section of the river he and Karen had looked out to the day before. He imagined the sound of church bells, the wet leaves on Esplanade. He and Karen were working on something here. Either they had figured it out correctly or they hadn't. Luck was something he thought about, always worried about. If you gambled, you needed it, and he wondered if this was the main reason he gambled at all because he believed it was the only way luck could find him. But he also knew that waiting for it could make a person desperate. When Karen had called Leo a few days earlier to tell him about the fix, he supposed one of the things she didn't have to say was that they were each desperate in their own way, that other people had edged ahead of them because these were the people who understood exactly how luck worked.

When it was time, Leo pulled on his windbreaker and extract-ed the messenger bag from the middle drawer. He used the inside pocket of the windbreaker for her cash, then split his own stash, stuffed some into each of the side pockets and zipped all the pockets shut. He dug in a pocket of the messenger bag, pulled out some rubber bands, and stuck them in the back pocket of his jeans. The rubber bands were for collecting, and he always liked to carry a few. Whenever he cashed a decent ticket, he'd fold the bills twice, put a rubber band around them, tuck them away. That was house money; he should hang on to it, save it for another time. He couldn't remember when he'd started this routine. The rubber bands said he expected to collect at the windows. Why would he ever stop carrying them?

He began his walk for the Fair Grounds. Sunlight played through the trees and cool air touched at his neck, the backs of his hands. First post wasn't for a couple of hours, but the simulcast parlor would be open. Races from tracks further east were about to start. He heard a woman's voice singing from inside a house across the street, like something from a musical. Up ahead stood a bar— "Big Show Lounge" the sign said—and though he hadn't been thinking about a drink, he decided to duck inside, have a quick beer. Behind the bottles of liquor, one wall was filled with win photos from the Fair Grounds, some in black and white. A guy in a postal worker's uniform, the shirt unbuttoned, sat further down the bar counter with half a shrimp po-boy and a bottle of Miller beer in front of him, and it all looked good to Leo. When the bartender nodded at him, Leo said he'd have the same. He glanced up at the *CNN News* on the bar's TV, and after the bartender brought him a beer, Leo drank it so quickly that the bartender brought him another bottle without Leo asking. Twenty years ago, he might've dreamed of being in a spot like this one, and in this way Leo wanted to feel like things had actually worked out all right. He had a pile of money with him and was about to bet a race where he had a big advantage. If a younger version of himself could've looked into the future and seen this moment, that younger self would've thought, *All right, still in the game.* It seemed more obvious to him now how little he'd known then. Though sometimes you could get far while not knowing all that much; everything depended on whether or not you gave up. When his sandwich came, it tasted great and he tried not to wolf it down. He had all of his bets written on a folded piece of paper in his back pocket. He would play pick-3s, exactas, trifectas, daily doubles. He thought he could make that ten grand for himself and ten grand for Karen. It wouldn't be a killing. He wasn't sure he knew what that was anymore. Leo hadn't been a stupid kid; maybe if someone had sat him down and asked him what a killing actually was, he might've given it some thought before shrugging his shoulders. Just something to say. He was glad he could feel excited now, even if he wasn't certain about what might change. The counter began to fill with customers and he wanted to get going. The bartender stayed busy, so Leo left a $20 near his plate, said, "Man that was good," even though he didn't think anyone was listening.

7.

The walk to the racetrack lasted a couple of minutes and he passed the casino entrance, kept going until he reached the turnstiles for the grandstand. He paid his two bucks to get in, and the next thing he did was walk straight to an automated tote machine where he took money from the pocket with Karen's holdings and began to slide in twenties and fifties. He took the piece of paper with the written-down bets from his back pocket and glanced around before beginning to key those in. It was a mistake to look around, and he told himself not to do it again. He was a guy gambling at the track. He slowed down. He finished making a round of bets, tucked the tickets away, found a stand selling *Racing Forms*, bought one, asked the woman at the stand about the simulcasting parlor and she pointed. He walked through a set of glass doors, found himself outside again. In front of him was a peat-moss-covered horse path, one that led to the saddling area. He crossed over that, walked to another set of glass doors, and wound up in a big rectangular-shaped area with clean-swept floors and a long line of pari-mutuel windows. Seated at the tables at the far end were a couple dozen guys, black men. One guy was yelling loud at the wall of TVs—others were laughing at him. Leo took a two-person table for himself. The races were already going at Laurel Park and Thistledown, and he opened his *Racing Form*. People might've glanced in his direction, but it wasn't because he was white or that he was suspicious; they probably wanted to see if they knew him. He knew many of the players in Birmingham on a first-name basis but they didn't keep regular schedules. When they had money, when they could get away, they played. Some guys vanished for a while. Leo knew the players there but didn't ask them questions. "Good to see you," he liked to say when a familiar face stepped up to his window. The players who came to Birmingham were working class; many of

165

them worked outdoors, came straight to the track in their boots and coveralls. Like him, they didn't bet much. Small plays, slow death. Familiar faces meant you weren't the only one this was happening to.

Simulcast parlors offered TVs, betting windows, a coffee stand, a bar. Vending machine food. Racetrack management held a moths-to-light assessment of gamblers. They might as well have said to gamblers, *You need something to watch and somewhere to make your bets. Well, here it is. Don't ask for anything else.* Leo worked in a place like this. Six days a week, starting at 9 A.M. He'd go to his office on the second floor, check time cards, double-check schedules, then head downstairs to open the break room, wait for the tellers to arrive. He'd look over the plays he wanted to make for the day. When his tellers began to show, no one said much. There would be plenty of chitter-chatter at the windows. Leo would take a remote control out to the floor, check the schedule for the afternoon, and begin to set channels. Gamblers started to drift in at eleven. Before things became busy, Leo would stand at an automated teller and key in his bets. Along with his tickets, he kept a small notepad in his shirt pocket to record the post times of the races he was playing. If he worked behind a window, he had to watch from there, but if not he liked to walk out on the floor and stand with the other players. He tried never to let on whether he won or lost, though he imagined losing was obvious in his face. Then he would go back to whatever he'd been doing.

Of course, Karen could've gotten through this without him. She probably would've been able to slip out of the jocks' room, walk over here, make a quick bet on the horse she felt was going to win. It could've gone unnoticed. And if Leo said he couldn't come, she might have done exactly that. But he knew it made a difference to her not to have to do it. In her life, she already had a man who would savor the opportunity to do it for her. She left Vicksburg when she was a kid because she felt the moves she could make there would be limited. She left in order to become a jockey. She liked being a jockey, liked being in the saddle, guiding a horse along. She was older now, but she didn't want to feel older, not all the time. She hadn't lost control over everything.

Leo looked at the past performances for races at Laurel and Thistledown and went to an automated teller, slid in more hundreds, made more bets on Karen's race, tucked the tickets in pockets of his windbreaker. At one point, some in the simulcast parlor stood because the Fair Grounds PA system played the national anthem. Once that was done, the track announcer went over the changes for today's program. The horses for the first would be arriving in the paddock in a few minutes, and Leo thought about walking over there, standing at the rail, watching as Karen and the other riders emerged from the jocks' room. She didn't need to see him; she knew he was here. He stayed put, leafed through the pages of his *Racing Form*, checked out upcoming races at Aqueduct and Turfway. Then he went to the automated tellers again, slipped in money and keyed in bets for the first at the Fair Grounds.

Leo stayed in the simulcast parlor and watched the in-house feed of the horses parading in the paddock. Karen's horse, the five, was even money in the betting and there were good prices on everything else, including the four-horse, which stood at 9–1. The camera panned from one saddling stall to the next, and when it arrived at Karen's, she nodded as the valet, a tall man with a ponytail and a mustache, spoke in her direction. She smiled; maybe it was a good joke. She wore a helmet with a yellow cover, and her riding jacket had bright green and yellow stripes. Leo hoped she wasn't nervous; he hoped his presence here allowed her to focus on the race. Every race, be it fixed or straight, was a tricky enterprise. Everything happened fast and a rider's mind needed to be clear. The camera moved on to another rider, a ruddy-faced guy in red-and-black checkerboard colors. Post time was close, fifteen minutes away. Leo didn't have any bets left to make. No one was keeping track of what he did, he was confident of that, but if someone was, he wondered if he looked worried to them. The bets were fine, but when he'd seen Karen on the TV, he'd been rocked with a lot of feelings. He was helping her now, but how much had he helped with when they'd been together? Right after their marriage ended, he couldn't help but think the split had been his fault and that she was better off without him. In time, his view of their divorce had been modified. They loved horse racing, had escaped to it when they were young. They had spent much of their time together losing. Karen needed a better man than he'd been. He hadn't been a good husband, and the experience marked him because he didn't believe he could be. The minutes were passing; since he'd arrived at the track he'd been cool and focused, but now everything felt like a little too much.

He started to walk toward the exit since it seemed like the best idea. He pushed over a turnstile arm, made a right, and headed for the big grandstand lot, which was one-tenth filled with cars now, gamblers' cars, heaps, just like they drove in Birmingham. Leo walked out to the chain-link fence, wound up right where he'd stood this morning. He felt the breeze blowing in the direction of the finish line. The call of the race probably couldn't be heard from out here, not with the wind blowing like this. A man on a bicycle rolled by. He held a big can of iced tea in one hand and said, "What race is it?"

"First!" Leo said.

"Calvin in it?"

Calvin Borel, Leo guessed. He was riding at Oaklawn in Hot Springs this winter. "Not this one," Leo said.

"All right," the man said. He pedaled away. The horses for the first were in their warm-up gallops on the backstretch. It wouldn't be long now, just a few minutes. In the direction of the far turn, he noticed the dome above the trees, the cross atop it. How far away was that? It had to be beyond the statue of the Confederate general, the streetcar tracks. He had all the tickets zipped inside the pockets of his windbreaker. The horses had disappeared from the backstretch, and he supposed they were lining up in the gate now. The infield had a live oak tree that obscured the six-furlong pole; he could just make out the frame of the starting gate. He heard something from the stands, a little cheer, and he knew the horses had been cut loose and the race had started. The field of horses stayed knotted together, he couldn't tell anything, and a few seconds later a rider in white silks had steered his horse to the front. This was the four, Leo knew that. The field had sprinted for more than a furlong when Leo made out Karen's green colors; she was in the back but high in the saddle, fighting her horse. He could see that from where he stood, and then he felt himself blinking because it seemed as if the rider of the horse just to the inside of Karen popped up quick from his saddle and that horse dropped out of contention. Karen's horse began to pass one horse, then another. Leo thought he could hear the race-caller, but the field of horses bunched up again going around the turn. Out of the turn, the four stayed in front but Karen and Skyring were moving fast. When the horses pounded past Leo, Skyring's nose was right at the throat of the four. Leo had his hands gripped tight on the fence; he might've been shaking it. Skyring tore ahead of the four, pulled way ahead. Far down the stretch, Karen was the first to stand in the saddle; she'd arrived at the finish first. The other riders did the same when their horses hit the wire. Not one ticket in Leo's pockets was any good. He understood this. Fucking Karen! His mind flashed to an image the day before, when they were on the levee together. Had she been trying to warn him? He already knew this was a horse race. He walked fast along the hurricane fence, in the direction of the grandstand. He

169

could see the electronic oddsboard and he kept walking, saw the unofficial order of finish. The board said,

5

4

7

2

Above the "5," in blaring neon red, was the word "Inquiry." Leo stopped walking, laid his hands on the fence and tried to understand. His vantage point for the race hadn't been good, and he'd seen one rider take up pretty fast. On the oddsboard, the "5" began to blink.

Leo's hand had been stamped when he'd entered the track, so he showed that to the woman at the turnstile and she waved him through. He headed right for a TV set at the back of a mini-bar. The barkeep and the one player seated at the bar watched the TV screen intently and when Leo said, "What happened?" neither of them spoke. "Beer," Leo said. "Anything. What happened?"

"The winner's coming down," the bartender said without looking in Leo's direction. "What kind?"

"Bud," Leo said.

"We have Bud Light."

"Bud Light."

The TV screen showed a head-on view of the horses in the starting gate, and the horses broke from there in real-time speed. Skyring got out of the gate a half step behind the others. The four and the six drifted towards one another, and Karen guided her horse to the inside. Skyring wanted to run; the old boy was used to being in front. She tried to get him out of contention. After a furlong, she had some room, lowered herself on the horse, threw the reins at him, and Skyring ducked in, mashed the horse on the inside. The jock on that horse did all he could to stay in the saddle. Skyring started to roll then and Karen angled the horse to the rail again. They began to pass one horse, then another.

The TV screen replayed the sequence. When a horse was disqualified it was always placed behind the horse it had fouled; Karen's move was brilliant. He hadn't understood it when he'd watched the race from the parking lot. Her horse missed the break, which had been the plan. But it wanted to run; not having the lead apparently made Skyring want to run even harder. Karen couldn't fight the horse all the way around—everything would've seemed too obvious. The TV screen went to a shot of the oddsboard, where the "5" continued to blink. One could never be certain what the stewards would decide, and Leo held on to his beer. The placing-order numbers disappeared altogether. When illuminated again, the order went,

4

7

2

1

The track announcer's voice came on, said, "Ladies and gentlemen, due to interference, the unofficial race winner, number five, Skyring, has been disqualified and placed last. The official winner is…"

Leo felt as if he could swallow and he took a sip from his bottle. The payoffs were listed on the TV screen, and he understood that many of the tickets in his pockets were already winning ones. He'd have to go through them, one by one. The tickets together were worth twenty grand, maybe a little more. Leo decided to walk up a flight of steps and buy a seat in the grandstand; get something in a rear row. His *Racing Form* was still tucked under one arm, which seemed miraculous to him. He took a seat, opened the *Form*, and looked out to the oddsboard, which now listed odds for the horses in the second race. The payoffs from the first were still posted. The four horse had taken some money late, paid sixteen bucks to win. The exacta was worth eighty-seven dollars and twenty cents on the dollar; the one-dollar tri went for one hundred ninety-two even. That tri payout was low. The fixers had gone at it pretty hard. They wouldn't need to fill out an IRS form for any of this. Collect and go. Leo wanted to get interested in the second race; that would be the best thing right now. He had all afternoon to cash. For her win tickets alone, Karen would get eight thousand. She'd get a suspension for the ride she'd given on Skyring. Careless riding it would be called. But she'd performed like a wild woman to win the race. She couldn't be accused of anything else. Depending on the rider and the nature of the foul, suspensions could last from a few days to a week. Leo tried to imagine what she'd do with her time. Ride her motorcycle to Lafayette, find a place to stay for the meet at Evangeline. Maybe send some money home to her mother, who hated that Karen was a jockey in the first place.

Karen was safe for today. She had no other scheduled mounts this afternoon. She could ride at the next track without having to worry about a payback, not unless it came from the jock she'd almost sent over the rail a little while ago. The three-horse was the one she'd done that to; Leo checked his *Form*, saw the rider was Jerry Mesh, a journeyman with mediocre stats at the meet. No doubt in on the fix, maybe even dramatized things a bit by jumping high in the saddle like he had. But Karen had whacked him good. Leo had made some money for himself, had win tickets and exactas and trifectas in his pockets. There were daily doubles and pick-3s that still needed to play out. The plan had been for him to spend all afternoon here and he knew that he would. He tried to understand how much luck he'd already used. He could put a down payment on a new car. He turned the page to the second race. The horses were already on the track for that. In daily doubles, Leo had wheeled the four in the first with all horses in the second, so he was going to cash here no matter what happened. He felt like doing something more. The six looked good on the track, a big fit bay on its toes. Leo went back to an automated teller, slipped in one of his winning tickets, then bet two hundred to win on the six. Then he went over to a window where a live teller worked. He took one of Karen's tickets from another zippered pocket, and the teller counted out sixteen hundred and twenty bucks for him. He nodded to the teller, stepped away from the window. While walking back to his seat, he folded the money twice, wrapped a rubber band around it, dropped it back in the pocket that had Karen's holdings.

In the second race, the six broke well and stayed in close position until the top of the stretch. It made a move to take the lead, but then some longshot came along on the outside in the final yards and beat it by a head. Leo lost his win bet, but the daily double paid big; three hundred twelve bucks for a two-dollar ticket and Leo had five good tickets. His pick-3 tickets had been killed by the bomb that won the second, but he could live with it. He wasn't going to sit here and play five or ten bucks a race when he had just made thousands for himself. Karen probably imagined him sitting in the stands now and doing this very thing. He was the guy she remembered, but there was more to their marriage than that now. If, back when they were married, she had let him in on a race like this and they'd collected on it like they had today, he would have bought champagne and laughed with her about how easy things were and how they were going to be even easier. He thought of his own future now, though it didn't have to do with where he wanted to go with the money he'd just made. Leo didn't want to look back at this day and think of it as the day he'd blown the money he and Karen made on a fixed race. So he would tuck some away. He would eventually go through all the money because he was a guy who never stopped believing a huge payoff was out there. He didn't have to stop believing that. Not believing it might have been too much, especially for someone like him. He understood he was better off not believing it right now, though. He wasn't going to sit here and play five bucks a race, but to bet recklessly would be to ignore what he and Karen had just pulled off.

His main goal for the remainder of the afternoon became not to lose all that he had made. He turned a page, looked at the entries for the third, picked a horse, bet two hundred to win on a longshot and then cashed another of Karen's tickets, put her money away. His horse in the third never hit a lick. He lost the fourth and fifth races, kept his play at two hundred per and then, in the sixth, he caught something, a 5–1 shot in a mile race on the turf. The horse had only run once before, but that race had been on a dirt track in Chicago and the horse's pedigree screamed for the grass. Leo collected over twelve hundred for this play and decided to tip his bets to four hundred per. He lost the next four races; his picks were nowhere close to winning. With one race to go, he figured he'd lost back about a thousand all told. The final race, a sprint for Louisiana-bred maidens, had a big field of twelve, and he watched the post parade and wondered if he ought to skip betting the race and just go out, stand at the fence where he'd been for Karen's race, try to appreciate something. He thought, *Fuck that, I appreciate plenty.* He looked at the *Form* for a couple minutes more, decided on the two, bet a thousand to win on it. The horse he bet made a little run down the stretch but was nowhere close to winning.

At the end of live racing there were clouds in the sky, and the color made him think of blue cotton candy. He had a couple of tickets left to cash for Karen. He went back to the simulcasting parlor to do this and then stood at the TVs there, considered playing the sixth at Golden Gate or the third at Zia Park. Somebody said in his direction, "I can't see Turfway!" and he moved away, decided it was time to go. He walked along Esplanade, hit the bodega, picked up a can of Miller High Life, a pint of Dewar's, beef jerky, and a roll of breath mints. He let himself into the house, went up to Karen's room, set the grocery sack on the dresser, then began taking the bands of money from his windbreaker. He thought about leaving them out for her to see, that he had cashed her tickets just this way. He decided she didn't need to know his rubber-band system. She still had to meet Thunderbird at the Starbucks. Leo took away the bands, unfolded all of her winnings, and placed the money in the drawer she had taken it from the night before. Just over eleven thousand. He stuck the pint of Dewar's in his messenger bag; that was for the train ride home. After that, he waited for her to call. He sat on the edge of the bed, looked out the window and sipped from his beer. The sun had been setting, and the color of the light out on the street kept changing. Leo wanted to sort through the ideas running through his head, and one of them was that he was sorry this was over. He would've been happy to do it all again tomorrow. Instead, he would be taking the train back to Birmingham and he tried to imagine how he'd feel then. The Crescent line ran from NOLA to NYC, and the train ran late because the freight trains had the right of way. On the way over, he hadn't thought of calling Amtrak to check about this and as a result had spent two and a half hours waiting at the Birmingham station. He'd looked over the past performance sheets, and by the time the train arrived he felt like he had a handle on how things would go. He had a row of seats to himself, and once he'd set the sheets down he'd watched the small towns and empty brown fields pass by. He had wondered if he and Karen would make love. He wasn't sure how he'd feel when he first saw her. The motorcycle ride through the city streets in the rain had been very good. They weren't confused about anything.

8.

When he first sat down on the edge of the bed, Leo had felt like talking to someone, but the longer he sat there the less he felt this way. The sky turned dark, the streetlights came on. His phone rang and he hoped it was Karen and when he checked he saw her number. After he said hello, she did practically all of the talking, said the meeting with Thunderbird had gone all right, that he'd smiled at her, said he appreciated her quick thinking. He'd paid her with two one-thousand-dollar bills and she was standing in the produce section at a Rouse's Grocery right now and did Leo want anything? Leo said not really and she said she needed to get to sleep tonight, not stay up late, and that she wanted to exercise horses in the morning like normal. After he hung up, Leo said, "Okay, Jesus. You don't want to sleep with me. I get it." His eyes went to the window. He decided to turn on the radio.

Karen opened the door to the room a little while later. He was sitting up in bed reading a few-days-old edition of the *Times Pica-yune*, had the radio tuned in low to the college station. A little while ago, he'd heard a young woman singing a cover of "The Boxer." He wanted to tell Karen about it. She had a green Rouse's shopping bag and carried it over to him, took out a pint of Cutty. Leo stood, walked to the dresser, held up the pint of Dewar's he'd bought, and they laughed. He stuck the Dewar's back in his bag and said, "Lemme see those thousands." She reached for her pocket, held them out. He took one, held the ends with both hands. "These are fairly cool," he said. "How'd you pay for the food?"

"Debit card. Lose anything back today?"

"A little."

"I thought I'd split this with you."

"No. Here, take it. Here." She did. "I didn't have to deal with Thunderdome or whatever his name is."

"Come on, have a drink," she said. "I brought up two glasses from the kitchen, I'll join you." She left the bag on the bed.

"Your cut's in this drawer," he said. He sat on the bed and put together the drinks. He poured himself three fingers, her two.

She closed the drawer. "See how easy that was?"

"I'm guessing old Skyring felt like running today. That was incredible what you did."

"You're getting carried away, Leo."

"No one can accuse you of not wanting to win."

"He ran like he did because he thought I was gonna buzz him. I didn't, though. After the break, I wanted to rein him in. But he wouldn't settle down. I had to make an adjustment. In the other races, he ran good. But man, he ran even better today. That's a shame. He was way the best. Maybe he doesn't need that buzzer."

"Next time you ride him you'll find out."

"Oh, the trainer fired me already," she said.

"That's no good."

"Horse starts losing again, he'll put me back on him. They're going to Evangeline."

Leo held up a glass for her. She accepted it. "Does the Thunder guy suspect you bet?"

"Didn't ask him about what he suspected," she said. She sat next to him. "They made their money, that was the point of it all. You watch the tote, keep an eye on their patterns?"

"Sure. I want to make love to you."

"Leo."

"I wanted to say it at least."

She nodded. "Okay."

"Okay, you might?"

"Okay, I understand." She took a drink from the glass. "I mean I'm a winner. Everyone wants me." She closed her eyes, opened them. She glanced in his direction, seemed interested in the details of his face. She said, "My goal overall is not to be bitter," she said. "That's been true for a long time now. How am I doing?"

"Good."

"I'll feel sexy tomorrow. Right now, I'm beat. How about it Leo, you gonna be bitter?"

In a second, he said, "No."

"No?" she said.

"I didn't get a *Form* for tomorrow, though."

"There's one in the bag there."

"Seriously?"

"No." She laughed. "I'm not your wife, you know." She finished her drink and stood and walked over to the dresser, set the glass there. She began to undress. She got into bed wearing her underwear. On his side, he had the old newspaper on his lap. The bag she'd brought home was still at his feet. She turned her back to him, stuck her behind against his hip. "Now we're married," she said. She laughed. He guessed they both were exhausted.

He waited a minute, listened to the music from the boombox. "You all right, Karen?"

She sighed. "I don't know. I feel good and then I don't."

"You eat?"

"I ate."

"You felt good about everything, you'd be a fool." He thought for a time. "I certainly wouldn't have anything to do with you."

She pushed up against his hip. "You're funny."

He drew in a breath. He said, "I don't feel perfect today." He felt as if he wanted to say more. But he could not figure out what to say exactly. "We get the Evangeline feed at Birmingham," he said. He lay still. He thought he could feel her breathing in and out.

"You said that already."

"I like to think of that money in your drawer there as alimony."

"You're being silly tonight."

"I know I am."

"I'm going to go to sleep in a few minutes. What time's your train leave?"

"Seven."

"I'm gonna have to drop you off early if you don't mind. I gotta go to work."

"I don't mind." He glanced at the newspaper on his lap. "I'm gonna read this for a while. Light bother you? The music?" She didn't answer. He picked up the paper. He had the local news in front of him and he read the stories on the first page, then opened the section and read some more while the bottle of Cutty rested against his thigh. He took a sip, then another. At one point, he awakened with the lights on in the room, music still playing. It had been indie-folk; now it was garage-band. Karen didn't stir. He got up quietly, turned things off, undressed down to his underwear. He slipped under the covers, lay on his back, scooted over just enough so that his hip touched against her.

He awakened with her stroking him. He felt her breath against his cheek. "It's time," she said. "You ready?" He didn't speak. She got on top of him, the bed creaked, the headboard tapped at the wall. She reached for it. They changed positions, the headboard tapped louder and they got down on the floor, brought the bed covers with them. They lay on the covers afterward. She said, "I wanted this, when it was all done."

"No matter how it turned out?" She didn't answer and he said, in a whisper, "Everyone in this house is probably having sex. Sid and Nancy are probably down there thumping all night. We had to be quiet about it?"

"Yes," she said. "Sid and Annie."

"Okay," he said.

"Let's lie here for one more minute," she said. "Then, we gotta get going." She sniffed, said, "How did I feel?"

"Great."

"I think we can stop by the track kitchen and get you a *Form* for today."

"You don't have to do that."

"I think we should, Leo."

"I can go a day without a *Racing Form*."

"Well, I don't want you riding on that train all morning thinking about how much in love you are with me."

"Yeah, we wouldn't want that."

Her voice was quieter when she said, "Come on, time to go."

Karen didn't have an extra helmet, but she felt he ought to wear something, so she insisted he put on the ballcap he'd worn when they'd ridden through the rain. The houses on the street were dark and there were dry leaves on Esplanade, though he knew live oaks were that way, their leaves falling around the end of winter. The ride took just a minute; the track kitchen was an oblong building made of cinder blocks and painted white, and she pulled up to the entrance. She switched off the engine and he stayed on the seat of the motorcycle while she went inside. A few minutes to five his watch said, which meant a two-hour wait at the terminal. Beyond the roof of the kitchen the night sky looked blue-green, and he thought he could see clouds in it. Karen carried out a folded *Racing Form* and had already flipped down her visor. He wished he'd asked for a coffee because track kitchens made it strong. Instead, he unzipped his bag, tucked the *Form* in there, zipped it up, and placed his hands on her shoulders. Karen steered them through the empty streets. They passed under pools of yellow-gray lights made by the streetlamps. The traffic lights all blinked yellow, and she only had to slow occasionally on their ride to Loyola Avenue. Near the entrance to the terminal were a couple of parked taxis, their drivers leaned up against the passenger door of the taxi in front. They held cigarettes and one nodded to Karen and Leo as they went by. A very good motorcycle, Leo thought. He hoped Karen held on to it.

After they rolled to a stop, he stepped off while she stayed on. In something of a spontaneous move, he leaned forward and kissed her helmet and, after he stepped back, she sped away. She hadn't said anything about the cap, and he kept it on as he walked toward the terminal entrance. Inside, it seemed as bright as it had been when the train brought him here. It was good that the terminal wasn't a shadowy place. The gift shop and the visitor info booth were closed.

A handful of people were scattered about in the seats of the waiting area. He went to the vending machines, looked them over, and decided to hold off. He took a seat, one that had plenty of space between himself and the other person in the row. A young guy with fair skin and a crew cut, probably military. The guy wore earphones and his head bobbed lightly. Leo wondered what he'd do with the money he'd made. He decided he wouldn't take the *Racing Form* from the messenger bag until he could think of a few things at least. He glanced over to the guy with the headphones. The guy noticed Leo looking at him, pointed to Leo's ballcap, gave a thumbs-up. In the windows near the ticket booth were the reflections of the people sitting in the waiting area. Beyond all that, everything looked black. Leo had reached a moment in his life where he didn't want anything. He didn't have to take out the *Form* just yet.

THE END

181